Rupert Street Lo[nely Hearts Club]
&
Boom Ban[g-A-Bang]

D0757264

This volume brings together two gloriously bittersweet plays from the award-winning author of *Beautiful Thing* and *Babies*.

'Harvey has just about the most natural ear for authentic-sounding comic dialogue of anyone of his generation . . . still ridiculously young and talented, Jonathan Harvey is now becoming seriously good.'
Independent

Rupert Street Lonely Hearts Club
At 15 Rupert Street, Dean is in love with Marti who is in love with Shaun who is in love with Juliet who is in Barbados. Meanwhile, George is in love with Malcolm who has left and Clarine just loves Jesus and Zoë Wanamaker. Welcome to the Rupert Street Lonely Hearts Club.

Boom Bang-A-Bang
Kentish Town. Eurovision night, 1995. It's Lee's first Eurovision party without Michael, joined instead by a small but far from select gathering of friends. As the atmosphere heats up, recriminations and revelations fly, and there will be blood, sweat and tears before the voting of the Belgian jury.

Jonathan Harvey comes from Liverpool and now lives in London. His plays include: *Cherry Blossom Tree* (Liverpool Playhouse Studio, 1987) which won him the 1987 National Girobank Young Writer of the Year Award; *Mohair* (Royal Court Young Writers Festival, London/ International Festival of Young Playwrights, Sydney, 1988); *Tripping and Falling* (Glasshouse Theatre Company, Manchester, 1989); *Catch* (Spring Street Theatre, Hull, 1990); *Lady Snogs The Blues* (Lincoln Arts Festival, 1991); *Wildfire* (Royal Court Theatre Upstairs, 1992); *Beautiful Thing* (Bush Theatre, London, 1993 and Donmar Warehouse, London/ Duke of York's Theatre, London, 1994), winner of the John Whiting Award 1994; *Babies* (Royal National Theatre Studio/Royal Court Theatre, 1994), winner George Devine Award 1993 and Evening Standard's Most Promising Playwright Award 1994; *Boom Bang-A-Bang* (Bush Theatre, 1995); *Rupert Street Lonely Hearts Club* (English Touring Theatre/Contact Theatre Company, 1995). Television and film work includes: *West End Girls* (Carlton); *Love Junkie* (BBC); *Beautiful Thing* (Channel Four/Island World Productions).

by the same author

Beautiful Thing
Babies

for the complete Catalogue of Methuen Drama titles write to:

Methuen Drama
Michelin House
81 Fulham Road
London SW3 6RB

Jonathan Harvey

Rupert Street
Lonely Hearts Club
&
Boom Bang-A-Bang

Methuen Drama

Methuen Modern Plays

First published in Great Britain in 1995
by Methuen Drama
an imprint of Reed International Books Ltd
Michelin House, 81 Fulham Road, London SW3 6RB
and Auckland, Melbourne, Singapore and Toronto
and distributed in the United States of America
by Heinemann, a division of Reed Elsevier Inc
361 Hanover Street, Portsmouth, New Hampshire NH 03901 3959

ISBN 0 413 70450 5

A CIP catalogue record for this book is available from the British Library

Typeset by Wilmaset Ltd, Birkenhead, Wirral
Printed in Great Britain by Cox & Wyman Ltd, Reading, Berks

Contents

Rupert Street
Lonely Hearts Club

Rupert Street Lonely Hearts Club was first produced by English Touring Theatre and Contact Theatre Company. It opened at the Contact Theatre, Manchester, on 27 September 1995 prior to a run at the Donmar Warehouse, London, with the following cast:

Shaun	Scot Williams
Marti	Tom Higgins
George	Lorraine Brunning
Clarine	Elizabeth Berrington
Dean	James Bowers

Directed by John Burgess
Designed by Jackie Brooks
Lighting by Gerry Jenkinson

With thanks to Angela Clarke, Karl Draper, Suzanne Hitchmough, Morgan Jones and Andy Serkis for the first draft reading at the Royal National Theatre Studio.

Characters

Shaun, *twenty-three, a pretty, straight lad from Liverpool.*
Marti, *thirty-three, his louder, camper, elder brother.*
George, *lives downstairs to Shaun. She is in her late twenties and from Kent.*
Clarine, *twenty-eight, quite portly. She has a repertoire of different personalities, and although she is from Kidderminster, she speaks usually in either a London or a Rochdale accent. Lives upstairs to Shaun.*
Dean, *twenty-six, a friend of Marti's. Broad London accent.*

Setting

The play is set in Shaun's bedsit, east London, in the spring of 1995.

There are two doors, one the main door leading to the landing, the other leads to the kitchen. There is a big sash window stage left with a rafia blind over it. There is a three-quarter bed stage right, and centre stage a settee with stretch covering and matching chairs. A coffee-table sits between the three. There is a gas fire, plants, a phone, standard lamps and a chest of drawers. On the wall are various posters, and a mirror. The feel is youthful, slightly bohemian and occasionally ethnic. Front of stage there is a telly and video and a music centre.

Note
An oblique/stroke within a speech serves as the cue for the next speaker to overlap with the first.

Act One

Scene One

In the dark before the lights come up, the opening of Jam and Spoon's 'Right In The Night' plays loudly. As the music fades, the lights come up gradually on **Marti** *and* **Shaun**, *pissed in the middle of the afternoon.* **Shaun** *is in the right armchair,* **Marti** *on the couch. There are bottles of wine on the coffee-table, finished and unfinished, a bottle of Jack Daniels and they each have a glass.* **Marti** *and* **Shaun** *are reciting the cheque scene from* Mildred Pierce, *with* **Shaun** *playing Mildred (Joan Crawford) and* **Marti** *playing Veda (Anne Blyth). They start speaking before or as soon as the lights start to come up, and the music fades underneath their voices.* **Marti** *is wearing PVC trousers, and a big baggy mohair jumper. Importantly, his hair is shaved to a number two all over. (M) indicates an impersonation of Mildred, (V) an impersonation of Veda. Sitting in the left armchair, nursing a big bottle of water is* **George**, *who is not drunk, but a bit bewildered by their venomous display.*

Shaun (*M*)   I've never denied you anything. Anything that money could buy I've given you. But that wasn't enough, was it? All right, Veda, from now on things are going to be different.

Marti (*V*)   I'll say they're going to be different. Why d'you think I went to all this trouble? Are you sure you want to know?

Shaun (*M*)   Yes.

Marti (*V*)   Then I'll tell you. With this money I can get away from you.

Shaun (*M*)   Veda!

Marti (*V*)   From you and your . . .

Shaun (*prompting him*)   . . . chickens . . .

Marti (*V*)   Chickens and your pies and your kitchens! And everything that smells of grease. You think just because you made a little money . . .

Shaun   You've skipped a bit!

Marti Shut up. (*V*) . . . you can get a new hairdo and some expensive clothes and turn yourself into a lady.

George This is amazing.

Marti (*V*) But you can't, because you'll never be anything but a common frump whose father lived above a grocery store and whose mother took in washing.

Shaun (*M*) Veda! Give me that cheque!

Marti (*himself*) I haven't finished yet!

Shaun (*M*) I said give it to me!

Marti (*himself*) I haven't . . .

Shaun (*M*) Get out, Veda.

Marti (*himself*) I haven't slapped you.

Shaun (*M*) Get out before I throw you out. Get out before I kill you.

Small Pause.

George Wow, that's like, pretty emotive stuff.

Marti It's also completely wrong. It's (*M*) 'Get out, Veda. Get your things out of this house right now before I throw them into the street and you with them. Get out before I kill you.' (*Himself.*) actually.

Shaun Fuck off, Marti.

Marti (*imitates him*) Fuck off, Marti.

Marti *and* **Shaun** *giggle. The last bicker reminds* **Shaun** *of something and he launches straight into a scene from* Whatever Happened to Baby Jane? *He's playing Blanche (Joan Crawford).* **Marti** *then plays Jane (Bette Davis).*

Shaun (*B*) Oh Jane I'm sorry. I didn't mean to ring for my breakfast. I was just wondering who all those people were at the back door.

Marti (*J*) It wasn't anything.

George Oh, I've seen this one.

Marti (*J*)   Just that nosy Mrs Bates going on about your picture last night.

Shaun (*B*)   Oh, really? Did she like it?

Marti (*J*)   Oh, really? Did she like it? She liked it.

The lads laugh.

George   I have. I've seen that with Malcolm.

Shaun (*à la Bette Davis*)   Enjoying yourself?!

Marti   Malcolm?

George   Isn't that the thing about the two feuding sisters, one of whom's a wheelchair/user?

Marti   Wheelchair-bound./yeah.

George   Malcolm loved that/flick.

Marti   Joan Crawford's confined to a wheelchair/in it.

George   Oh, now come on, Marti, wheelchairs are liberating, not confining.

Shaun   Sort yer nouns out,/Mart.

George   What was that movie called? Malcolm adored/it.

Marti   Who the fuck's Malcolm?

Shaun (*to* **George**)   *Whatever Happened to Baby Jane?*

Marti   She's here and she's thirsty. (*Helps himself to another drink.*)

George   Malcolm's my ex.

Shaun   He dumped her.

Marti (*raising his glass*)   To Malcolm. A man with taste. Oh, but it's so passé that movie now. Everyone's got their hands on it. But only us two know the cheque scene from *Mildred Pierce*. I weaned him on it, didn't I?

George (*getting up*)   You'll have to forgive me. I'm having terrible cystitis.

Shaun (*screams*)   Get out! Get out before I throw you out! Get out before I kill you!!

George   Right.

George *exits awkwardly.*

Marti   God, how big's her bladder?

Shaun   You heard what she said.

Marti   Christ, I've never known anyone go the loo as much as her.

Shaun   You don't know the first thing about the female anatomy, do you.

Marti   I know this much. Your little friend's near bored the slingbacks off me.

Shaun   Her heart's in the right place.

Marti   Her mouth isn't, she talks shite.

Shaun   She's Juliet's friend really.

Marti   Oh, so you can't stick her.

Shaun   She lives downstairs. She's all right.

Marti   Your girlfriend's got dodgy taste in mates, that's all I can say. Who else does she knock about with? Eva Braun?

Shaun   It was you that asked her in! She only came round to pick up a knitting pattern.

Marti   What's she trying to knit herself? A sense of humour?

Shaun   She's nice enough.

Marti   She's a cunt.

Shaun   Didn't you know that word's offensive in polite company?

Marti   Polite company? Where d'you think you are? The Ritz? God, that girlfriend of yours has really got to you, hasn't she.

Shaun   She's got a name.

Marti I remember a time when every single one of your sentences was prefixed by the word fucking. Now look at you. Cast adrift in a sea of political correctness. This is offensive. That's offensive. I tell you what *is* offensive. Your hair's offensive.

Shaun There's nothing wrong with my hair.

Marti What d'you wash it with? Lard?

Shaun Ah, you're just on one now.

Marti And with every right. God knows what your customers must think. You're hardly a walking advertisement for hairdressing. Must be like getting your eyes tested by a blind man. Or is that offensive? Ah, who gives a fuck.

Shaun You, for some reason.

Marti I forked out five hundred quid for that van. If you're gonna go all camp on me and run a mobile hairdressers then I'm entitled to give a fuck. Get it washed! (*Slaps him over the head.*) If you mess this business up while Juliet's away.

Shaun I love getting pissed with you. You just stand there ragging me . . .

Marti You deserve it.

Shaun . . . and telling me things I already know like I haven't washed my hair.

Marti I have a degree in ragging. A double degree with campery. Don't knock it, it's a lethal combination.

Shaun There's no such thing as a double degree. It's joint honours.

Marti Oh, you think you know it all coz you've got your City and Guilds in hairdressing and you've done a bit of a business course at night school. (*Joan Crawford.*) Well, you don't, and you never will!

Shaun You can't stay here all day, you know.

Pause.

Shaun I'm cutting someone's hair at six.

Marti   God, you really live life in the fast lane, don't you.

Shaun   Oh, I'm sorry, I don't sell stretch covers./I can't be . . .

Marti   There's nothing wrong with selling stretch covers.

Shaun   There is if you're a twat.

Marti   Fine. If you don't like my stretch covers then you don't have to have them disgracing your sumptuous first-floor apartment.

Marti *starts clawing at the cover on the couch to get it off.*

Shaun   Oh, you always have to get the last word.

Marti   No no, it's quite all right.

Shaun   Marti!

Marti   I can take a hint.

Shaun   Oh, come on, Marti . . . Marti! Marti!!

Shaun *scrambles over and wrestles with* **Marti** *over the stretch cover.* **Shaun** *trying to get the cover back on,* **Marti** *trying to get it off.*

Marti   No. If you don't want it . . .

Shaun   I do.

Marti   You've just . . .

Shaun   Put it . . .

Marti   Eh?

Shaun   Just leave it on!

Marti   All right, all right!

Shaun   Sit down.

Marti   Okay. Jesus. What's got into you?

Shaun   Nothing.

Marti   Eh?

Shaun   Sit down, Marti.

Pause. **Marti** *sits down.* **Shaun** *stays standing behind the couch, holding onto it for support.*

Marti   What's up? Cat got your tongue?

Small pause.

Marti   Well, here's a clue then. 'I'm sorry I insulted your job.'

Shaun   I'm sorry I . . .

Shaun *goes and sits on the bed, head in his hands fighting tears.*

Marti   Oh, Christ. Young love! (*Tuts.*) If you're looking for sympathy you'll find it in the dictionary between shit and syphilis. (*Tuts.*) D'you think she's crying in Barbados?

Shaun   Of course she's crying. She's burying her grandad.

Marti   She hardly knew him.

Shaun   He's still her grandad.

Marti   She was brought up over here.

Shaun   You're so racist.

Marti   Am I fuck racist. I know Juliet, she'll be a tower of strength to people she hasn't even met. She'll be a shoulder to cry on. She certainly won't be sitting in a messy flat feeling sorry for herself.

Shaun   I told her I wouldn't look at another woman while she was away.

Marti   So?

Shaun   The first woman I meet and I'm talking to her.

Marti   George? But she's a mate of Juliet's.

Shaun   When I went the chippy.

Marti   Oh, so you can't talk to someone in the chippy now? How else are you supposed to order? Sign language?

Shaun   No. When I come back, coming up the stairs. This new bird's moved in upstairs. We chatted like. She's coming later. I'm gonna do her hair.

Marti   Oh, aye? On the make, is she?

Shaun   I hope not. She's a dog.

Marti   Well, what you worried about then? God, you get yourself into some states. You never used to be like this.

Shaun   I can't help it, Mart.

Marti   It's all right, lad.

Shaun   Have you ever felt like this?

Marti   Ooh, well . . .

Shaun   No funny voices.

Marti   Course I have, doll. Who hasn't? But . . . this is your first time. Oh, I know you've notched 'em all up on your bedpost, but even I can see it's different with Juliet.

Shaun   It is, man, it is.

Marti   It's just . . .

Shaun   What?

Marti   You've got to be in control of your feelings. Don't relinquish it to some other twat. Oh, I'm a bitter old queen, I know, but I've had a lot o' knocks, haven't I? Been let down more times than a lilo. When you get to my age you don't expect anything. Then what you do get is a bonus.

Shaun   I told her I wouldn't have chips.

Marti   Your cooker's on the blink. We've all got to eat.

Shaun   I tried sticking me fingers down me throat after I'd had them, like she used to, but it only brought up bile. (*He holds up a stained pillow.*)

Marti   Oh, you soft get. Come here. (*Goes and sits on the bed with him and hugs him.*) I should be slapping you really. You're just pissed.

Shaun   I'm not.

Marti   Sometimes being a bit down, Shaun, it's just God's way of showing yeh you're human.

Shaun   Who you being now? Mrs Overall?

Marti   I'm being serious. D'you feel really low?

Shaun (*shrugs*)   I just miss her.

Marti   I mean, you don't feel like doing anything daft, do yeh?

Shaun   Like what?

Marti   I dunno.

Shaun   Like killing meself?

Marti   No, I didn't mean/that.

Shaun   Yes you/did.

Marti   Well, it's best to check. I mean, it's happened before in the family.

Shaun   Thanks a lot, Mart.

Marti   I didn't think you did, you know.

Shaun   No?

Marti   It's actually er . . . it's actually a counselling technique. The Samaritans are trained to say that in every call.

Shaun   Are they?

Marti   Yeah. Not that . . . I've ever rung them or anything. Seen it on . . . on a documentary or something.

Shaun   I have.

Marti   What?

Shaun   Rung them.

Marti   Have yer? (**Shaun** *nods*.) So have I. See, we're all daft, aren't we.

Shaun   What did you ring 'em for?

Marti   Oh, this was years back. I got crabs and didn't know what to do.

Shaun   Did they tell you?

Marti   Oh, yeah. They even rang back a few days later to check they'd gone. When did you ring?

Shaun   Last night.

Marti   You shoulda rung me.

Shaun   You were out.

Marti   Well . . . d'you feel like going back to Liverpool?

Shaun   Gotta look after the business.

Marti   You could take a few days off surely.

Shaun   I'll be all right.

Marti   It might do you good to get back home.

Shaun   I am home.

George *enters. She impersonates Maggie Smith in* The Prime of Miss Jean Brodie.

George (*Scottish*)   I am a teacher. First, last and always. And you will never sack me. And I will never resign. (*Beat. Herself.*) Jean Brodie.

Marti   Oh, we're not playing that one any more. *He's* cutting someone's hair.

George   Really?

George *goes and sits down.* **Shaun** *gets up and starts walking around.*

Shaun   Not at this precise moment in time.

Marti   Oh, forgive me.

Shaun   Six o'clock.

Marti   Oh, six o'clock. He's cutting someone's hair at six o'clock.

Shaun   It's a French pleat actually.

George   Right.

Shaun   So in fact there's no cutting involved.

Marti   God, I was way off the mark there then.

George   Who's?

Shaun   You what?

George   Who's hair are you cutting?

Marti   He's just told you he's not cutting anybody's hair!

Shaun   This new bird's moved in upstairs.

George   Oh, Zoë.

Shaun   Nah...

George (*to* **Marti**)   Zoë's an actress. From the television.

Shaun   Nah, I don't think...

George   Not that that impresses me, I prefer a good book. But I bumped into her by the umbrella stand and she certainly seemed okay to goodish I'd say. And actors often get involved in causes, don't they?

Shaun   No, the girl that's moved in up there's a singer.

George   I specifically recall her saying she was an actress.

Shaun   And her name's not Zoë.

Marti   Maybe you've got *two* people living upstairs. My, this is an interesting conversation.

George   We've got artists on top of us/Shaun.

Shaun (*to* **Marti**)   Well, why don't you say something interesting then.

Marti   I only say interesting things in interesting company.

George   Malcolm was pretty interesting. I used to say to him, 'Malcolm you are so interesting.' He just used to laugh.

Pause. **George** *notices all is not well.* **Shaun** *wipes his eyes and sits back in the armchair again.* **Marti** *gets a hanky out of his pocket and passes it to* **Shaun**.

Marti   Blow your nose. (*Cockney.*) The poor boy's missing his bitch.

Shaun   Don't be vile.

George   Dear Shaun, now you know how the other half lives. When Malcolm and I, as was, kinda you know, split up, I was a wreck.

Shaun (*to* **George**)   We haven't split up.

George   Bedtime was the big killer. What's the point of a double bed when you're all on your own? Why have a ratio of four pillows to one head? That's why I got rid of the double bed and got the single futon. They're so practical. And it makes a facking good easy-chair for the daytime. You can really experiment with it.

Shaun   I've been out wit loads o' girls before. Mad ones from Liverpool. Moved down here wit one o' them. Suppose I've never been wit no one as brainy as Juliet before.

Marti   That girl from your Saturday job was brainy.

Shaun   But Juliet blew me mind.

Marti   She'd got fourteen on *Screen Test*.

Shaun   I suppose I just miss having someone to bounce ideas off really.

George   Hey, Shaun. I make a great intellectual trampoline.

Marti   What was her name?

Shaun   I forget.

George   Honestly, while Juliet's away . . . well . . .

Marti   Tracey?

George   I'm only downstairs.

Shaun (*to* **Marti**)   No.

George   My door is always ajar.

Marti   She had red hair.

Shaun   Carmen.

George   There's always an extra vegeburger in my fridge of life for that unexpected pal.

Marti   She'd been on *Screen Test*. She showed us the video.

George   It's only fair. Juliet was a tower of strength to me when Malcolm and I, as was.

Shaun   It was Carmen.

Marti Was it? Who's Tracey?

Shaun Tracey worked in the pub.

Marti Did she?

Shaun Yes.

Marti Hadn't she been on *Screen Test*?

Shaun *Blockbusters*.

Marti That's it. That's who I meant. See? You always got brainy girlfriends.

Shaun Yeah but. Juliet's different. Brainy in a different way. Like . . . Like . . .

Marti The sex is better.

Shaun Yeah. No.

George Like you're in love. Right?

Shaun Nothing wrong with that, is there?

George It's . . . the tops. Isn't it?

Marti (*to* **George**)   Did you love him? Thingy?

Shaun Malcolm.

George Sure thing.

Marti Ah.

Shaun Are yer over it now?

George Oh, yes.

Marti Oh, good.

George I still ring him. Put on a silly voice. Pretend it's a wrong number. But that's just boredom really. Juliet was so good to me then, Marti, you know? She was fucking . . . right there. Yeah? Now that's the sign of a true friend, don't you think?

Marti Fair play to her, she's a brick.

George (*to* **Shaun**)   And if I could repay the compliment.

Shaun   But me and Juliet aren't splitting up. She's only gone for four weeks.

Marti   Yeah, well, George can keep an eye on yeh, Shaun. Can't you, George? Infidelity's in the genes in our/family.

Shaun   It's not in mine!

Marti   You'll keep an eye on him, won't you, George?

Shaun   I don't need looking after.

George   Actually, Shaun, I'm going out tonight if you fancy joining/me?

Marti   Where you/going?

Shaun   I don't think/so.

George   Oh, a departmental knees-up at a wine bar in Bow. The other English teachers have been haranging me to go for absolutely days.

Shaun   I'll stay in I think.

George   It won't be a late night. I'm going on a demo tomorrow in Welling so I'll have an early start. Shut the BNP. Hey, if you fancy coming to that.

Shaun   Well . . .

George   It's an important cause.

Shaun   I know it's an important cause.

George   I'm sure Juliet would jump at the chance/were she here.

Shaun   I know. It's just Marti's coming back here in the morning to chill out so I best stay in.

George   Oh. Going anywhere nice, Marti?

Marti   Just a fabulous bijou hole where they do a nice line in group sex in the bogatry.

Shaun   I hope you're careful.

Marti   God, I hope I am an' all. I can never remember. I'm that much off me face.

George   What . . . you actually have sex and stuff in those places?

Marti   Well, I don't pay an eight pound fifty entrance fee to do the cheque scene from *Mildred Pierce*.

Shaun   It's like a dark room.

Marti   We make it dark. First week we takes the lightbulb out and got stuck in. Second week they'd put a cage across the top o' the bogs so we couldn't reach the lightbulb. So this tranny takes her shoe off and jams the stiletto heel through the cage and smashes the bulb. Third week they'd put a perspex sheet across so the tranny gets a can o' black spray-paint out of her clutchbag and sprays it black. Instant darkness. Isn't she marvellous, George?

George   Cool.

Marti   I love that tranny. I'm meeting her there tonight.

Shaun   Have yer ever done it with her? Him?

Marti   Her. No. Sisters.

Shaun   What do they call her?

Marti   Fifi. Fifi Trixabelle La Bouche. Oh, Shaun, why don't you come out with us tonight? Ah, it's ages since we went out together, on our own.

Shaun   We wouldn't be on our own. Fifi Trixabelle My Hoop's gonna be there.

Marti   I've got six Es on me.

Shaun   I'm best off staying in.

Marti   Juliet'd love you going to a gay club. No temptation.

Shaun   Maybe another night.

Marti   Yeah?

Shaun   Yes.

George *gets up to go.*

Marti   Jesus, are you going the loo again?

George   Sadly not. I promised myself some meditation before
going out tonight so. Look, please don't think me rude rushing
off like this but . . . if you do find that knitting pattern I lent Juliet
. . . do come on down and knock on wood, so to speak. It's for a
Javanese-style skull-cap. It's got a picture of a woman on the
front, modelling one. A Javanese woman actually. It's just that
I'm going to knit some as end-of-term presents for my kids.

Shaun   Is it end of term soon?

George   No, but there are thirty kids in my class so I want to
get cracking on them a.s.a.p. Lovely to meet you, Marti.

Marti   And you. A rare/honour.

George   And I really appreciate the hospitality. I must repay
the compliment sometime. Wednesday?

Shaun   Er . . .

George   That's my quietest night marking-wise. (*To* **Marti**.)
I'm doing *Romeo and Juliet* with my Year Tens at the moment and
we're really beginning to crack it.

Marti   How clever of you.

George   Wednesday then. I've got this fabulous new recipe.
With aubergines. Bye.

Shaun   See you/George.

Marti   Trar,/doll.

George   Miss you already!

George *exits.* **Shaun** *pours himself another drink.* **Marti** *gets up and
goes around the room looking for something.*

Marti   Good shuttance.

Shaun   You can choose your girlfriend, but you can't choose
who lives downstairs to you.

Marti   You don't know anyone else.

Shaun   I know loads o' people.

Marti *has found* **Shaun**'*s hair clippers.*

Marti   Just coz you've cut their hair doesn't mean you've tested the bonds of friendship. (*Waggling the clippers in the air.*) Mow me lawn for me. I wanna look gorgeous tonight.

Shaun   Take your jumper off. I've got loads o' mates.

Marti   Name one.

Shaun (*tuts*)   Connor.

Marti   Now I don't want you laughing.

Shaun *gets a towel off the back of the door.* **Marti** *peels off his jumper. He's wearing a bondage harness.*

Shaun   I'm past caring, me.

Marti *sits on the couch.* **Shaun** *plugs the clippers in and puts the towel round* **Marti**'s *shoulders. He then proceeds to go over his hair with a number two on the clippers.*

Marti   Name another.

Shaun   You.

Marti   I'm your brother.

Shaun   Laurence.

Marti   Another. See? You can't.

Shaun   I can.

Marti   Well, go on then.

Shaun   All Juliet's mates. You don't know them.

Marti   When was the last time you seen Connor?

Shaun   Couple o' weeks back.

Marti   Laurence?

Shaun   I dunno.

Marti   Loner! It's a good job you've got me. It's people like you end up as serial killers.

Shaun   Oh, shut up.

Marti   I bet these walls are heaving with corpses.

Shaun   Only women and children. I'm very choosy about who I kill.

Marti   And then when you do let them in they're a waste of space.

Shaun   You being the prime example.

Marti   The prime example being that gang of skallies back home.

Shaun   There's nothing wrong with skallies.

Marti   Yes, but that particular bunch of skallies were a gang of twats.

Shaun   That was years/ago.

Marti   And you were one of/them.

Shaun   I don't see them any more.

Marti   You seen Jedda the last/time you were back.

Shaun   Jedda's all right really.

Marti   Tell that to his girlfriend.

Shaun   He doesn't see her any more.

Marti   She couldn't see him anyway with two black eyes. I'm surprised she could even find the baby half the time.

Shaun   Well, what about that gang of screaming queens you always had round the house?

Marti   They loved you.

Shaun   Me ma's wig went missing a few too many times for my liking.

Marti   At least they didn't go round beating people up coz they were bored.

Shaun   No, they just bitched people to death.

Marti   You're the one who ended up as a hairdresser, dear.

Shaun   You're never satisfied, are you?

Marti (*sarcastic*)   No.

Shaun   Would you be happier me doing something more macho?

Marti   You? You're camper than a big van! Why d'you think the queens loved you so much? Maybe you haven't got a woman coming round for a French pleat. Maybe it's a fella. Oh, who is it? Is it someone I know? Is it someone near to me?

Shaun   Yes. It's Ricky.

Small pause. **Shaun** *stops clipping.*

Oh, I'm sorry, Marti, it just slipped out. Oh/I am sorry.

Marti   That was a bit below the . . .

Shaun   It's just . . .

Marti   Okay, you're sorry. Drop it.

Pause.

Shaun   Come here. It's not even.

Marti (*looking in mirror*)   It's fine. It's fine.

Shaun   I'll just . . .

Marti   No.

There is a knock at the door. **Marti** *looks at his watch.*

Marti   It's six.

Shaun   Shit. (*To door.*) Hang on! (*Passes* **Marti** *his jumper.*) Put that on.

Marti   Oh, where's your sense of adventure?

Shaun   Barbados. Put it on, Mart.

Marti   Oh, you're determined to make me boring, you. Well, I refuse. I do. I simply refuse.

Shaun   Butch up or shut up, now which is it to be?

Another knock at the door.

Marti   I love a man who orders me about.

Slowly **Marti** *puts the jumper back on as* **Shaun** *opens the door to* **Clarine**. *She is dressed in a neon-blue seventies evening-dress and carries a guitar on a rainbow strap. She is speaking with a light, breathy, London accent.*

Clarine   Oright, darlin'? (*Laughs.*)

Shaun   Hiya, come in.

Clarine (*entering room, to* **Marti**)   Hiya.

Marti   Hiya. Fabulous frock!

Shaun   This is me brother Marti.

Clarine   Oh! Keep it in the family, yeah? Hello, babes, nice to meet you.

Shaun   This is . . .

Clarine   Clarine.

Marti   Like what they put in the swimming baths?

Shaun   D'you want a drink, Clarine?

Clarine   You're okay, darlin', don't wanna put you to any trouble.

Shaun   Ah, it's no trouble.

Clarine   Oh, okay then, a large one o' them'll do me fine thanks, love. Cor, got it nice in here, aint ya?

Marti (*passing her a Jack Daniels*)   Here you go, doll.

Clarine   Cheeky.

Shaun   Take a seat. French pleat.

Clarine (*giggles, sitting*)   You're a poet and you don't know. (*Remembers it's supposed to rhyme.*) It.

Marti   Can I have a look at your guitar, Clarine?

Clarine   Yeah, babes, you have a look at that, go on, you have a little play on that. Now . . .

Marti *takes the guitar from her. She is sitting on the couch.* **Shaun** *gets some Kirby grips out of a bag and starts messing with her hair, standing behind the sofa.*

Marti   When did you move in, Clarine?

Clarine   Oh, about three years ago now. I mean, days. I'm from Crouch End. Funny little place, init?

Shaun   Have you met George downstairs?

Clarine   No.

Shaun   Oh, she must've met your flatmate then.

Clarine   I haven't got a flatmate, darlin'. I'm on me own.

Marti   Have you seen *Mildred Pierce*?

Clarine   No.

Shaun   I wonder who she met then?

Clarine   I haven't met anybody apart from you, love. Maybe it was my mate who helped me move in. Maybe Mildred met her. She'll talk to anyone. It'll be her downfall.

Shaun   What's her name?

Clarine   Best Mate. (*Laughs.*)

Marti   I always wanted guitar lessons as a kid. Didn't I, Shaun? (**Shaun** *shrugs.*) Well, I did. But we were a bit strapped for cash in our family. I had piano lessons, for a while. Paid for them with me own pocket money. But the problem was, we didn't have a piano. So I used to have lessons on the table. Miss Burke, that was the piano teacher, she'd come round every Wednesday and draw the keys on the table in chalk and then we'd get cracking. I can still play 'Für Elise' even now. But after a certain stage she said it was pointless us carrying on. And me mother refused to buy us one. I mean, there was six kids in our family and they are pretty expensive, aren't they?

Clarine   Kids?

Marti   Pianos. I cried when she left the last time. Didn't I, Shaun?

Shaun   I wasn't born, was I?

Marti   Where d'you get it?

Clarine   The guitar? Oh, Jesus give me that. Yeah, wann'alf pleased.

Marti   Jesus?

Clarine   Jesus Christ. He's my best mate.

Marti   Kind of him, wasn't it? Generous.

Clarine   Well, when I say he give it me, he didn't actually give it me, he like, led me to it, if you like. I mean there I was groping around in the darkness for like, some sort of meaning to me life and a couple o' prayers later I'm in Hank's Music Store in Crouch End.

Marti   You're a Christian?

Clarine   I'm sorry but, I just love Jesus! (*Laughs.*)

Marti   So what, d'you play choruses on it?

Clarine   I only wish I could. See the only thing I can play is 'House of the Rising Sun'. But what I really wanna sing is 'Amazing Grace How Sweet the Sound'. I mean, I have prayed about, you know, acquiring the gift of playing by ear but. As of yet, no result. So, I have to make do with singing the words of 'Amazing Grace' to the tune of 'The House of the Rising Sun'.

Small pause.

And that's my act. Clarine Manger. Jesus was born in me! (*Laughs.*)

Marti   What, you just do the one number?

Clarine   And lead the people in prayer obviously. You've gotta have as many strings to your bow in the converting game. I'm down at the Kilburn Working Men's Club tonight. It's just my way of . . . spreading it about.

Shaun   Your hair's dead thick. This is gonna take ages.

Clarine   Oh, well. Must be a sign.

Small pause.

Marti. Can I just say, as a Christian, I feel it's right sad you
missed out on the gift of music. And that you were skint to your
last threepenny bit. And that your old girl couldn't summons up
enough love to buy you even a second-hand joanna. And well,
I'd like to take this opportunity to share with you both my gift.
And my joy, at having the Christ-child within me. By singin'.

Marti *hands her back the guitar quite guardedly.*

Clarine   No prizes for guessing the song though. D'you know
what I mean?

She strums a very long introduction of two chords.

Clarine   Usually I'd let the spirit move me and I'd be led in
some sort of choreographic format. But as I'm sitting down, I'll
skip that bit.

She continues with her intro. **Shaun** *is fixing her hair. Just as* **Marti**
*loses interest she begins to sing. She has a cookie, bar-room voice. She sings to
the tune of 'House of the Rising Sun'.*

Clarine (*sings*) Amazing Grace
                How sweet the sound
                That saved a wretch like me.
                I once was lost
                But now am found.
                Was blind but now can see.

*After a verse the lights fade. An instrumental version of 'House of the
Rising Sun' leads into the next scene.*

Scene Two

The next morning. **Shaun** *is in bed. The key goes in the door.* **Marti**
enters with coat and hat on accompanied by **Dean**. **Dean** *is dressed up as
Fifi Trixabelle La Bouche, glamorous sex kitten. His feminine get-up is
convincing, but he has the voice of a navvie. He carries with him a sports bag
and a lollipop-shaped Anti-Nazi League placard.*

Marti   Should I fly the kettle on?

Dean   Has he got any sounds?

Marti *exits to kitchen.* **Dean** *goes over to the stereo and switches it on. Morrissey is playing.* **Shaun** *wakes up.*

Shaun   Aright?

Dean   Oright? You aint got nothing better than this, have you?

Shaun   What?

Dean   I'm Dean.

Shaun   Aright.

Dean   You Marti's brother?

Shaun   Yeah.

Dean   Thought you was. You aint got anything with a better beat?

Marti *comes back in.*

Marti   Ah, sorry, doll, did we's wake yer?

Shaun   Yeah.

Dean   Ah, man, did we wake you up?

Shaun   Yeah.

Dean   Go back to sleep.

Marti   Shaun. Have you got anything else bar herbal tea bags?

Shaun   No.

Dean (*to* **Marti**)   Ah, man, listen to his accent. That accent is like, like literature. Books. The voice and that. Ah, man.

Marti   Isn't Fifi marvellous, Shaun?

Dean   Party on, d'you know what I mean?

Shaun   I'm gonna try and kip.

Marti   Ignore us, Shaun. We'll be quiet as church mice. Deaf and dumb church mice. In a very quiet church. In a very quiet town.

Dean   Eastbourne.

Shaun *lies back down and pulls the pillow over his head.* **Marti** *and* **Dean** *sit in the armchairs.* **Dean** *is still holding onto his placard.* **Shaun** *sits up.*

Shaun   Where d'you get that banner?

Dean   Downstairs.

Shaun   You soft get, that's George's.

Dean   I love this banner.

Shaun   Marti, put it back it's not funny.

Marti   No, I know. It's not funny that.

Marti *takes the placard off* **Dean**. **Dean** *looks around himself.* **Shaun** *lies back down.*

Dean   Nice pad.

Marti   Shares it with his missis.

Dean   Straight?

Marti   As a dye.

Dean   What colour?

Marti   Haemorrhoid-blue.

Marti *exits with the placard to go downstairs.*

Dean   Where is she?

Shaun (*not lifting head up*)   Barbados.

Dean   When did you realise you were straight?

Shaun   I dunno.

Dean   Right.

Pause.

Dean   Ere, mate. You got a bath or a shower or somin'? I gotta be in work by ten.

Shaun   Down the corridor. Second on your right.

Dean   Did you never fancy blokes?

Shaun   No.

Dean   Right.

Pause. Then **Dean** *gets his sports bag and goes to the door. He stands at the door looking at* **Shaun** *who is trying to sleep.*

Dean   I'm gon'ave a shower.

He exits and closes the door behind him. Knock on door. **Shaun** *drags himself out of bed, in only boxer shorts and a frown, and opens the door. It's* **Dean**.

Dean   You got a towel?

Shaun   In the bathroom. The red one's mine.

Dean   Can I use it?

Shaun   Yeah.

Dean   Ah, cheers, mate.

Dean *goes.* **Shaun** *shuts the door and gets back into bed. Knock at door.* **Shaun** *gets up again and opens it.* **Dean** *again.*

Dean   You got any shampoo?

Shaun   In the bathroom. Wash and go.

Dean   Soap?

Shaun   Yeah.

Dean   Eye make-up remover?

Shaun   Er, try the cabinet above the sink.

Dean   Cheers, mate.

Dean *goes.* **Shaun** *closes the door. On second thoughts he opens it and leaves it open. He gets into bed.* **Marti** *comes in with two lollipop-shaped Anti-Nazi League placards, leaving the front door open. He goes and sits down.*

Marti   Is that girl downstairs a lollipop lady?

Shaun *sits up.*

Shaun   Marti! Put them back!!

Shaun *angrily lies down and pulls the duvet over him.* **Marti** *however just sits there enjoying his placards. Presently* **Clarine** *comes in. She has changed her clothes. She wears brilliant-white tights, white Scholls, purple skirt, green top, red hair-grips. She goes and turns the telly on and sits down on the sofa.* **Shaun** *puts the pillow over his head. She gets the remote control and turns the volume up til it is deafeningly loud.* **Marti** *watches her incomprehensibly.* **Shaun** *sits up.*

Shaun   Oh, for fuck's sake, Marti!!

He sees it is **Clarine**.

Clarine   I like it loud coz I'm deaf in one ear.

She is now speaking with a Rochdale accent. **Shaun** *looks dumbfounded.*

Ask Miss Flaherty if you don't believe me.

Shaun   Clarine? D'you mind turning it down, girl?

Clarine   Ah, *Lost in Space* is on in a minute.

Shaun   Clarine?!!

Clarine   I wear goggles.

Shaun *gets out of bed and goes over to the telly and turns the sound down.* **Clarine** *looks at his semi-naked form in horror.*

Clarine   Mrs Flaherty! Mrs Flaherty! There's a man wi' no clothes on!!

He turns the music centre off.

Shaun   Clarine ...

Clarine   I wear goggles.

Shaun   What's to do wit yer voice?

Clarine   Don't tell 'em. You know what they're like.

Marti   Who?

Clarine   They'll put me in isolation.

Shaun   Eh?

Shaun *is flummoxed.* **Clarine** *gets up and puts the telly back on.* **Shaun** *looks to* **Marti**.

Clarine   I wanna watch me programme.

Shaun *sighs. He still hasn't woken up properly yet. He goes off to the kitchen.* **Clarine** *looks around the room.*

Clarine   Do they let you sleep in here?

Marti   Who?

Shaun *comes to the kitchen door pulling on a T-shirt.*

Shaun   Where d'you think yer are?

Clarine   Do they?

Shaun   This is my flat.

Clarine   Is it?

He goes back to the kitchen. **Clarine** *looks round her again. She starts to cry.* **Shaun** *comes back in.*

Marti   Took too many drugs?

Clarine   I think I'm in the wrong place.

Shaun   Your flat's upstairs.

Clarine   Where am I?

Marti   Fifteen Rupert Street.

Clarine   Rupert Street? That's where I'm going.

Shaun   No, love, that's where yer are.

Clarine   I know you two.

Shaun   I'm Shaun. I done your hair last night. This is Marti, you know Marti.

Clarine   I get dandruff, do you?

Shaun   No.

Clarine   Why?

Shaun   I use Wash and Go.

Clarine   Why?

Marti   So he doesn't get dandruff.

Clarine   Why?

Pause. This is freaking **Marti** *out. He looks extremely suspicious.*

Shaun   Last night you had a cockney accent.

Pause.

Clarine   Me mam's name's Elsie. She lives in Belle View Heights. Will you take me there?

Marti   Take her there, Shaun, go on.

Shaun   What's your name?

Clarine   She's got a bloke called Phil. He works for Hargreaves.

Shaun   But what's your name?

Clarine   Lucky.

Shaun   Yeah?

Clarine   He were our dog.

Shaun   Your name.

Clarine   Joyriders got him.

Pause.

Marti   I'm twatted.

Clarine   Is that a Welsh name?

Pause.

Shaun   D'you wanna go back to your flat?

Clarine   Belle View Heights?

Shaun   No. Upstairs.

Clarine   I wet the bed. Promise you won't tell. You know what they're like. (*Looks at telly.*) Ah, look, *Lost in Space*! Can I have t'sound up?

Shaun   Not today.

Clarine   Oh. Oh, okay then.

Clarine *watches telly.* **Shaun** *goes into the kitchen.*

Clarine   This int *Lost in Space*, it's *Aap Kah Hak*!

She gets up and goes to the door, not to leave but to feel secure. **Shaun** *returns with a cup of tea.*

Shaun   I've got yer a tea here.

Small pause.

It's herbal.

Small pause.

Clarine.

Pause.

Shaun   It's not Clarine, is it? Is it Zoë?

Clarine   Zoë Wanamaker.

Shaun   Is that your name?

Clarine   I'm in *Love Hurts*.

Marti   Have some tea.

Clarine   I'm gorgeous.

Pause. He then walks over to her and gives her the tea.

Clarine   Will you take me back to Belle View Heights?

Shaun   D'you know where it is? Is it in Manchester?

Clarine *shakes her head.*

London?

Shakes her head.

Is your mum there?

Clarine   It doesn't matter. I cut me finger before. I thought I'd got a stone in the sole of me shoe but it was glass and I tried to pull it out. Look.

Marti   Ooh, that sounds nasty. Doesn't that sound nasty?

She shows them her finger.

Clarine   I'm in Rupert Street, aren't I?

Marti Yeah.

Clarine Fifteen. Top flat. I best be getting back, me mam'll wonder where I've got to.

Shaun What's your name?

Clarine Me mam's calling me.

Shaun Look, there's a launderette down the road. You turn left out of here and it's by the lights. If you wanna wash your sheets.

Clarine Right.

Shaun *smiles at her. She goes, taking her tea with her.* **Shaun** *sits on the right armchair.*

Marti Is she barmy?

Shaun Dunno.

Marti Is she tripping?

Shaun Maybe she is on drugs.

Marti D'you think she's got any left? Oh, go up and ask her for me.

Shaun You go to bed.

Marti Can I take me lollipops?

Shaun Nah, I'll take them down in a minute.

Marti Fair enough.

Marti *gets into bed.*

Shaun Crash eh?

Marti Okay, I'll crash.

Dean *comes in with a red towel wrapped round his waist and carrying his sports bag.*

Dean Cor, my mouth feels like the bottom of a birdcage. Had a cockatoo in there last night.

Dean *starts to dress with clothes from the bag. Gradually he puts on a McDonald's uniform and cap.*

Shaun   D'y'ever watch a programme called *Love Hurts*?

Dean   These trousers. Bit tight round the crotch.

Shaun   Do yeh?

Dean   No. Man and woman together? Turns my stomach.

Shaun   Was there someone in it called Zoë?

Marti   Zoë Wanamaker.

Shaun   Is she pretty?

Dean   Well, you'd probably think so, seeing as how you're into pussy. And she's got a certain feline wotsit to her.

Clarine *appears at the doorway holding bedsheets in her hands.*

Shaun   Clarine. The launderette's downstairs. Out the front door and turn left. It's by the traffic lights.

Marti *looks up.*

Clarine   Right.

Clarine *goes.*

Shaun   D'you work in McDonald's yeah?

Marti   Night night. (*Settles down.*)

Dean   Yeah. Got a problem with that?

Shaun   No. But a mate o' me girlfriends. He went in McDonald's. Or it mighta been Kentucky Fried Chicken. Anyway, he asked for a chicken burger with no mayonnaise.

Dean   That's simple enough to do, you just miss the mayonnaise out.

Shaun   But he when he bit into it, he got a gobful of really sour mayonnaise.

Dean   Mistakes happen. It's a stressful job.

Shaun   Anyway, turned out it wasn't mayonnaise. The chicken had a cyst. And he'd bit into it.

Dean   Wouldn've been McDonald's.

Shaun   I think it was.

Dean   It weren't McDonald's.

Shaun   Maybe I'm getting mixed up.

Dean   And maybe your mate's a lying little toe-rag. It weren't McDonald's. Impossible.

Shaun   I'll bow to your better judgement.

Dean   You veggie?

Shaun   Vegan.

Dean   D'you know what gets me about vegetarians? What vegetarians seem to forget is . . . if it weren't for meat, right, there'd be millions more unemployed. You take a look at the news. We got, what, three million unemployed?

Shaun   More or less.

Dean   Yeah, well, if you vegetarians got off your fat arses and ate a bit o' meat instead o' being a bunch o'no-hope ponces, you'd be putting people in work. So I think you better think again before you start ramming paranoia down people's throats.

Shaun   I don't impose my views on anyone.

Dean   Good. Coz no cunt'd listen to you. This country's fed up of people like you. Do this, do that. You're a bunch o' champion wankers. No offence.

Pause.

We should go out for a pint with your missis away.

Shaun   Yeah?

Dean *moves over to the bed.*

Dean   I don't mind straight places. High Holborn (*Shaking* **Marti**.) McDonald's, you can reach me there. (*To* **Marti**.) I'm getting off, Marti. Oright?

Marti   Sweet boy.

Dean   Gonna go for a pint with your kid brother this week.

Marti   Didn't we have a great time tonight eh?

Dean   Blinding. (*To* **Shaun**.) Later, boy. (*To* **Marti**.) See you, mate.

Marti   See yeh, doll.

Shaun   See yeh.

Exit **Dean**.

Shaun   Marti, don't go to sleep just yet.

Marti   I've gotta watch these drugs.

Shaun   You had a buzz, yeah?

Marti   You would tell me if it was getting out of hand, wouldn't you?

Shaun   I'm always telling you.

Marti   I was the Belle of the Ball in them bogs last night.

Shaun   Marti, I'm a bit worried about Clarine.

Marti   God help me if they ever found out I was so big in stretch covers.

Shaun   Marti.

Marti   Let's never fall out again. I know I'm on E but. Let's never fall out again. I'm glad we're mates now.

Shaun   Okay.

Marti   Promise.

Shaun   Aren't you worried about Clarine?

Marti   Promise?

Shaun   I promise.

There is a knock on the (open) door and **George** *pops her head round, then comes in.*

George   Not interrupting anything, am I? I was just . . . well, I'm going to Welling. Hi, Marti. And I wondered . . .

Marti   Hiya!

George   . . . if you'd seen . . . oh, there they are.

She gets the placards.

For the demo.

Shaun   I'm sorry, George. Marti's mate brought them up.

George   Oh, that's okay. Just thought I'd check and see if you'd changed your mind.

Shaun   No.

Marti   Them banners are gorgeous.

George   Made them myself from a special kit.

Shaun   Sound.

George   But you don't fancy it?

Shaun   I'm a bit knackered.

George   Right, well, I'll go and fight facism alone then. Have a good time last night, Marti?

Marti   Heavenly.

George   Great. See you later then.

Marti   See yeh.

George   Ciao Shaun. Take care. Looking forward to Wednesday.

George *exits with her placards.*

Marti   Wednesday?

Shaun   Marti, I think we need to talk about Clarine.

The lights fade. Patsy Cline's 'Come On In (And Make Yourself At Home)' plays us into the next scene.

Scene Three

A few days later. **Shaun** *is sitting on the couch with a glass of red wine. Another glass of red wine sits on the coffee-table, along with a stack of plates.* **George** *stands wiping a plate with a tea towel, looking out of the window. She looks to* **Shaun**, *but he's in his own little world. She searches for conversation.*

George   Did you know these windows are reinforced?

Shaun   No.

George   Well, they are. Redlich had them all reinforced triply about a year ago. All the large ones. In case of break-ins.

Shaun   Yeah?

George   He didn't however reinforce the kitchen windows. Now if you were a sneak-thief intent on burgling this place, which window would you go for? I know which one I would, the kitchen. It's much smaller. Much less mess. Typical.

Shaun   What?

George   Our capitalist bloody landlord.

Marti *comes in from work, suit and brief-case. He chucks the brief-case on the bed and sits in the right armchair. He holds a bottle of white wine.*

Marti   Hiya, girls.

George   Marti, hi.

Shaun   All right?

George   Dinner won't be long. You look tired.

Marti   You'd look tired if you'd been up the Ideal fucking Homes exhibition trying to sell the delights of stretch covers. Still I managed a lunch-time drink in the Coleherne where I was besieged by a plethora of angelic skally trade. Managed to club one into submission and drag it back kicking and screaming to the exhibition centre. Did I fuck. (*Passes* **Shaun** *the wine.*) Cabernet Sauvignon, get it opened.

Shaun   Tar.

George *is putting the plate on the coffee-table.*

George   Now. Cutlery.

Shaun (*getting up*)   I'll do it.

George   You sit down. Relax. It's about time someone pampered you.

Shaun   I can get the cutlery for God's sake.

Shaun *takes the bottle into the kitchen.* **George** *is admiring the stack of plates.*

George   Juliet has such great taste in plates. D'you think she got them from Africa?

Shaun (*off*)   I got them!

George (*to* **Marti**)   They're so ethnicy.

Shaun (*off*)   From Brick Lane market!

George   Temper temper! (*Laughs.*) Sometimes he reminds me so much of Malcolm it's untrue.

Shaun (*off*)   I'm not a bit like Malcolm!

George   Well. No. It's just. He had great taste in plates too. He used to say, 'George, I know they only get covered in food. But hey, a plate's a plate.'

Marti   How long were you going with him for?

George   Three weeks and a morning. (*Beat.*) But the emotional intensity was on a par with at least a six or seven monther. Juliet agreed.

Shaun *enters with knives and forks and a glass of wine for* **Marti** *and two open bottles of wine on a tray. He puts the tray on the table, then passes* **Marti** *his glass.*

Shaun   There.

Marti   Ooh, we didn't do City and Guilds in Hostess Skills, did we?

Shaun   I'm not the hostess. She is.

George   I just thought it'd be a nice treat for you. To have someone cook for you. A house meal. And have people round. And you not to have to lift a finger. And you not to have to even leave your own flat.

Marti   He's just got things on his mind, that's all.

George   The cooker?

Shaun   What? No.

George   That is the landlord's responsibility.

Shaun   Have you got an atlas?

George   Yes.

Shaun   Can I borrow it?

George   I don't mind cooking it downstairs. It's no problem. Actually, don't you think, while I'm checking the food and grabbing that atlas, it'd be a good idea to ring Redlich and tell him about your Smeg?

Marti   I beg your . . .

George   Cooker. Smeg Cooker. I know that's what Juliet would do.

Shaun   Yeah, I know that's what Juliet would do, but I'm not her, am I?

George   Is there a problem with you and Juliet?

Shaun   No!

George   Oh. Oh good. Hey I'm really looking forward to having a chat with Zoë. Aren't you?

Shaun   Er . . .

George   (*heading for the door*)   I can imagine we're all going to bond furiously.

Marti   Haven't you told her?

Shaun   George, I don't think her name is Zoë really.

George   You don't?

Shaun   No. In fact I know it isn't.

George   You have been doing your homework. Stage name? Great!

George *exits.* **Marti** *bursts out laughing.*

Marti   You kill me, you do!

Shaun   Leave it out, will yeh?

Shaun *reaches for the phone. He gets a number out of his Filofax and dials it. It's a long number.*

Marti   Why the fuck didn't you tell George?

Shaun   Because I'm not in the mood for all this if you must know.

Marti   Who you ringing?

Shaun   Never you mind.

Marti   What d'you want an atlas for?

Shaun   What d'you think? (*On phone.*) Hello? Hello, can I speak to Juliet, please? (*Pause.*) Juliet Ransome? (*Pause.*) Oh. (*Pause.*) Shaun. (*Pause.*) Bye. (*He puts the phone down.*)

Marti   Why don't you just tell us all to piss off? It'd only be putting into words what your body language is screaming.

Shaun   All right then. Go on, piss off.

Marti   Not on your life. I wouldn't miss this for the world.

Shaun   See? What's the point?

Marti   The point is people are trying to help you.

Shaun   And I'm just trying to sort me head out.

Marti   It's just a few people. A few hours. Some good cooking and a bottle o'wine. By the time you slip into bed tonight believe me, your head will be sorted.

Clarine *enters in her evening-dress from the first scene. She's still speaking in her Rochdale accent.*

Clarine   Hiya.

Marti Hiya, love. Er. Why don't you sit down and. Can you drink?

Clarine White wine.

Marti *pours her a drink*.

Clarine I hear things are afoot in Kilimanjaro. It wouldn't surprise me if we were all raped in our beds.

Shaun Listen, girl. (**Clarine** *sits down on the sofa beside him*.) You know George?

Clarine George?

Shaun She thinks you're Zoë Wanaker.

Clarine I'm not though.

Shaun Yeah. I know that.

Clarine It's Wanamaker, not Wanaker. (*Tuts*.) As in, 'I wanna make 'er happy, but I can't.'

Marti But you're not. You're not her.

Shaun And you told her you were.

Marti And we think you should tell her you're not.

Shaun Or d'you want us to tell her?

Marti (*to* **Shaun**) *You* to tell her!

Clarine Can't *she* tell her?

Shaun Who?

Marti (*to* **Shaun**) You'll have to.

Clarine I believe there are grave misgivings in Poulton-le-Fylde. Leaves on the track, it's the road to ruin.

Shaun We've got to decide on a name for you. Just for tonight.

Clarine I can't tell you me name, it's not allowed.

Marti Well, can you make one up?

Clarine Can I?

Shaun Yeah.

Clarine   Really?

Marti   Yes!

Clarine   Oh, there's so many to choose from. Juliet!

Marti   No. Not Juliet.

Shaun   My other half's called Juliet.

Clarine   You?

Shaun   Me girlfriend.

Marti   What's your favourite name?

Clarine   Shaun.

Marti   No, that's his name.

Clarine   It's my favourite name.

Shaun   Yeah, but it's a lad's name.

Clarine   Well, she's called George.

Marti   What about Clarine?

Clarine   We don't speak.

Shaun   Oh, come on.

Marti   Yeah, hurry up or I'll make one up for you.

Shaun   A name!

Clarine   Grace.

Shaun   Sound.

Clarine   Amazing Grace!

Marti   Well, Grace it is then.

Clarine   Just keep reminding me in case I forget.

Marti *gets up and hands* **Clarine** *her wine. He strolls round the room.*

Clarine   Thank you.

Marti   I take it Juliet still hasn't rung. (**Shaun** *shakes his head.*) Well, maybe she's skint.

Shaun   What d'you know about anything?

Marti   Well, many's the time I've been away and wanted to ring fellas but me wallet's been empty.

Shaun   What, fellas like Ricky? Rich Ricky from Rain Hill?

Marti *puts his foot on the arm of* **Shaun**'s *chair. He's wearing Doc Martens.*

Marti   You see that? That's steel toe-capped that is. And d'you know what? If you don't shut up about ... Ricky ... you're gonna have a lovely impression of this steel toe-cap ... just ... (*Runs his fingers over* **Shaun**'s *forehead then pokes him.*) there.

Shaun   I'm shitting meself.

Clarine   I've done/that.

Marti   Oh, I would be if I/was you.

Clarine   Not at a/party, mind.

Shaun   If she is skint, there's such a thing as reversing the charges.

Marti   She's only been gone a week. Give her a chance.

Clarine   I like parties.

Shaun *gets up and goes to the kitchen.*

Marti   We all like parties. (*Sits back in right armchair.*) Except the Conservative one.

George *enters with atlas.*

George   I'll second that. (*Puts atlas on table.*) Five minutes foodwise, okay, everybody? Zoë! Hi! So glad you could make it! (*Kisses her on each cheek.*) Well, that's the way you thespians do it, isn't it?

Clarine   Mm.

George   What an amazing dress!

Marti   Er, which school is it you teach at again, George?

George   Crown Street Comp. Turn left at Toys 'R' Us and it's staring you straight in the face. So, Zoë, tell me, been on the telly lately?

Clarine   No.

George   Actually I have a terrible admission to make. I don't actually possess a TV. I mean, don't get me wrong, I'm not anti-TV. No way, I think it's great. I really do. It's just that you are looking at a total Bookworm with a capital B. And I just know, that if I had one, that'd be it. I'd be hooked. I'd watch everything. Even soaps. Actually . . .

Marti   What is it you teach again, George?

George   English.

Marti   Oh, yeah. So that's as in, the language.

Goerge   Yeah, that's right.

Marti   That's great, yeah.

George (*to* **Clarine**)   I'm doing *Romeo and Juliet* with my Year Tens at the moment and I really think I'm finally getting somewhere. Great piece.

Marti   Oh, he's fantastic that Shakespeare.

George   Actually, I mean, don't tell anyone. It's not that I'm . . . oh, it sounds so silly. Two of my Year Eights have nominated me for the *Smash Hits* Teacher of the Year.

Marti   Oh, brilliant, George. Oh, you must be made up.

George   It's very embarrassing. Have you done much Shakespeare, Zoë?

Clarine   No.

George   Right. So. More contemporary stuff, yep?

Marti *shouts through to* **Shaun**.

Marti   Shaun! George has been put up for Teacher of the Year!

George   *Smash Hits*.

Shaun (*off*)   Brilliant!

George   Don't tell anyone. (**Shaun** *comes to door*.) Well, you can tell Juliet, if she rings.

Shaun   Could you, er, give us an 'and in the kitchen, doll?

Clarine   I can give you two. (*Gets up.*)

Marti (*raising his glass*)   Up yer bum and no babies.

Shaun (*to* **Clarine**)   Come 'ed.

Shaun *leads* **Clarine** *into the kitchen.*

George   She has got an amazing dress sense. She's so outrageous! I just wouldn't have the gall to wear something like that. D'you know what I mean? Hey, Marti?

Marti   What?

George   Cheers.

Marti   Cheers.

George   You know, you really remind me of my great mate, Pete. You've got exactly the same sense of humour. I must introduce you to him actually coz I think you'd probably get on really well. He goes to the L.A. D'you ever go there?

Marti   No, I think it's vile.

George   Right. I think he does too actually.

Marti   Well, it's pointless him going then, isn't it? Life's too short to surround yourself wit vileness.

Geroge   Right. Well, I think it's handy for him. Five-minute walk from his flat and stuff.

Marti   If there's one thing I despise in people it's laziness.

George   You wanna meet my Year Nines.

Marti   No thanks.

Shaun *and* **Clarine** *come back in.*

Shaun   George?

George   Aha?

Shaun   Can you just come in the kitchen a second?

George   Sure. (*Gets up. To* **Marti**.) Won't be long.

George *exits with* **Shaun**. **Clarine** *still standing. Pause.*

Clarine   D'you think she'll ask me to leave?

Marti   She's cooked yer a meal, hasn't she?

Clarine   I'm going.

Marti   Oh, don't go. Our Shaun's really on a downer at the moment. The more people here, the more it takes his mind of his girlfriend. Please. Just for him.

Clarine   I like him better than George. I only liked her coz she thought I was Zoë Wanamaker.

Marti   She only thought that because you told her.

Clarine   I need the toilet.

Clarine *exits.* **Marti** *lights up a cigarette.* **George** *returns with* **Shaun**.

Marti   She's gone the loo.

George   This is all rather . . .

Shaun   You weren't to know.

George   It's so sad. Erm. Dinner should be ready now, so . . .

George *exits via the main door to go down to her flat.*

Marti   What did she say?

Shaun   Why?

Marti   What did she say?

Shaun   Does it matter?

Marti   God, what's got into you?

Shaun   I've told her, all right. That's all that matters. (*He pours himself a drink, unnerved by* **Marti**'s *sudden silence.*) She didn't say/ nothing.

Marti   I don't wanna know now.

Shaun   I'm just sick of the third degree.

Marti   Oh, grow up.

Shaun   I'm sick of you.

Marti   Oh, the bitchy stakes are rising, I like it. Come on!

Shaun   Shut up.

Marti *launches into the girdle scene from* All About Eve, *playing Margo Channing (M), hoping* **Shaun** *will take the bait and do his Birdie impersonation.*

Marti (*M*)   You bought the new girdles a size smaller. I can feel it.

Shaun   Oh, God.

Marti (*more insistent*)   You bought the new girdles a size smaller. I can feel it.

Shaun   Oh, that's right, drag out Margo Channing. When the going gets tough resort to *All About Eve*.

Marti   You can't remember it.

Shaun   I don't want to remember/it.

Marti   You've forgotten/it.

Shaun   How could I forget/it?

Marti   You/have!

Shaun   The number of times you made me sit down and watch it over and over and over again till it was drilled into me skull. And every other scene. One day we were saying 'Hail Mary' at the end of school and I came out with the girdle scene from *All About Eve*.

Marti   You have forgotten it!

Shaun   You're not listening to me, Marti. Will you just shut up and listen to someone else for once in your life?

Marti   You/have.

Shaun   Oh, for God's sake.

Marti (*M*)   You bought the new girdles a size smaller. I can feel it.

Pause.

You bought the new girdles a size smaller. I can feel it.

Shaun *relents awkwardly, impersonating Birdie (B).*

Shaun (*B*)   Something maybe grew a size larger.

Marti (*M*)   When we get home you're going to get into one of those girdles and act for two and a half hours.

Shaun (*B*)   I couldn't get into the girdle in two and a half hours.

Pause.

Marti   We keep throwing you a bone, Shaun, trying to lift you out of this. George is doing it now, cooking you a meal. I'm trying me hardest. Snap out of it, darlin'.

Shaun *starts to cry.* **Marti** *stubs out his half-smoked cigarette.*

Marti   Oh, I can't do a thing right, can I?

Pause.

I promise I'll never make you do *All About Eve* again. From now on the names Margo Channing, Eve Harrington . . . whoever . . . they're all banned in this flat. Okay? *Mildred Pierce, Baby Jane,* banned. Are you listening to me?

Pause.

I done all them things, made you say . . . all them things . . . coz . . . well, coz I . . . coz you were me favourite brother. I practically brought you up. Where was me dad most nights? Down the boozer and quick mouthful of abuse when he got back. Not that you'd've known, you were in your bed by then . . .

Shaun   I knew.

Marti   You were only in bed coz I put you there. And where was me mam? Doing petty jobs like carrying boxes to keep us in grub and him in ale. Who spent half their life writing notes to your teachers, cooking you beefburgers, cleaning your bloody PE kit? And what did I get out of it? Christ, it was the biggest day of me life when I got that video knock off from Big Mary. We were the only house in the street wit one. Didn't mind bringing in your mates to show it off. Didn't mind bunking school to watch porn videos with them, did yeh?

Shaun   I'm not saying . . .

Marti   Don't you throw back in my face all I've done for you. You've done it once and I won't let it happen again. D'you hear me?

Shaun *tries to wipe his eyes as* **George** *enters. She sees he is upset.*

George   I just thought you should know. There are some very strange noises coming from your toilet.

Marti   I'll go and check.

Marti *exits.*

George   Dinner's ready. Smells good.

Shaun   I'll be all right in a minute.

Pause. The sight of **Shaun** *crying has moved* **George** *to modest tears.*

George   Last time I cooked this was for you-know-who.

Shaun   Take no notice of me.

George   Shaun. Do you mind if I . . .?

She goes to hug him.

Shaun   Why?

George   Well, if Juliet was upset.

Shaun   No, George, it's not . . .

George   I'm not trying to . . .

Shaun   What?

George   Hug?

Shaun *smiles. They hug. She is keener than him.*

George   Thanks.

She kisses him once on the lips. **Shaun** *is surprised.*

George   Sorry.

She returns to just hugging him. Just then, **Marti** *and* **Clarine** *enter.* **Marti** *coughs to announce their presence.*

Marti   She thought she was in a space capsule.

Clarine   I forgot.

George   If I don't get downstairs none of us is ever going to eat.

George *exits.* **Clarine** *sits on the couch.* **Marti** *eventually sits in the right armchair.*

Clarine   How far away's Kidderminster?

Shaun   I don't know.

Marti   If you'd like us to go and leave you two to it, please say. Light a couple of joss-sticks, get Joni Mitchell on the CD, you'll be well away.

Shaun *laughs sarcastically.*

Marti   You can do better than her.

Shaun   I already have.

Clarine   Is it near Birmingham? Kidderminster?

Shaun   You've got it all wrong as per.

Clarine   Where's Birmingham?

Shaun   In the Midlands.

Marti   I'm only saying.

Shaun   All right lad.

Marti   Don't call me lad you straight bastard. Call me girl, or doll, or love. Takes years to get this camp.

He goes in his pockets for something. Gets cigarettes out.

Clarine?

Clarine   Zoë.

Shaun   Grace!

Marti   Oh, I don't care what your name is, d'you want one or not?

Clarine *shakes her head.* **Shaun** *is looking round the room for his ashtray.*

Marti (*to* **Clarine**)   No offence doll, but my brother's always been hopeless at finding the right people to surround himself with.

Shaun   Oh, and I suppose that Polish fella you used to knock about with was the ideal friend, was he?

Marti   I can't help it if I'm generous.

Shaun   He took you for every penny you had!

Marti   I can't help/being generous.

Shaun   What was his name?

Marti   I've grown up/since then.

Shaun   Maybe if I said I needed a fortnight in the sun to sort me head out you'd/come up with the readies.

Marti   I forked out . . . I forked out for that van of yours, didn't I? More fool/me.

Shaun   More fool me for accepting it. You remind me of it every five minutes.

Shaun *slams the ashtray he has found in* **Marti***'s lap*.

Marti   Hey, watch the crown jewels. I'm sitting on a small fortune here.

Clarine   Have you ever been to Birmingham?

Shaun   He probably has. He's been everywhere.

Marti   Not by choice.

Clarine   What's it like?

Shaun   Yeah, what's Birmingham really like, Marti. I've often wondered.

Marti (*tuts*)   It's got a fabulous gay scene but I don't think much to its Bullring. You've got an atlas there. Why don't you show her where Birmingham is?

Clarine   I didn't really want Birmingham. I wanted Kidderminster.

Marti   Well, why have cotton when you can have silk?

Enter **George**, *followed by* **Dean**. **Dean** *is dressed to kill, in men's clothes.*

George   Look who I found skulking about in the lobby.

Marti *bursts out laughing.*

Dean   Oright?

Marti   You're timing's brilliant, Dean.

Shaun *nods a hello.*

George (*to* **Marti**)   Isn't it?! Grace, would you like to fetch an extra plate from the kitchen and get an extra glass? Dean's going to stay for dinner. You'll find them on the side.

George *exits.*

Clarine   Right.

Dean (*to* **Clarine**)   Cheers, mate.

Clarine   I'm Grace.

Dean   Right.

Clarine *exits to kitchen.*

Shaun   Did you know Marti was going to be here?

Marti   No, he didn't.

Dean   Thought we could go for that drink.

Shaun   Bit of a dinner party going on.

Dean   Don't let me stop you. (*Sits on couch.*)

Marti   You know my little brother's straight, don't you, Dean?

Dean (*to* **Marti**)   If you must know I come round coz I lost your number. Thought I could get it off of him.

Marti   I believe yeh. Thousands of highly intellectual people would be in two minds.

Clarine *enters with plate and glass.*

Clarine   I did it.

Marti   Oh, well done, girl. Give her a round of applause.

Marti *claps.* **Clarine** *puts the plate and glass on the table.* **Shaun** *fires an imaginary pistol at* **Marti**. **Clarine** *pours* **Dean** *a wine.*

Marti (*to* **Shaun**)   I'm not scared of you, yeh know.

Dean   Aint you got no lager?

Shaun   No.

Dean   You got a problem with me being here?

Shaun   No.

Dean   Well, put a smile on your face then, you miserable cunt.

Clarine (*horrified*)   That's not allowed.

Dean   What?

Clarine   The 'c' word. It's not allowed.

Dean   You some sort of feminist?

Clarine   I'm Grace.

Shaun (*to* **Clarine**, *passing her the atlas*)   Look. Kidderminster.

Dean   I understand that some women find the word cunt offensive. Personally the word don't offen me, but the thing does.

Clarine   Does that really say Kidderminster?

Shaun   Yeah.

Marti   You'll have to tell Shaun a few jokes, Dean. He hasn't been feeling to good.

Dean   Aint ya?

Shaun   Would you with a brother like that?

Enter **George**.

George   Now I need a big strong man to give me a hand upstairs with the hostess wagon. Marti? Would you do the honours?

Marti (*getting up, to* **Shaun**)   With friends like you, who needs enemas?

Shaun   You're not original, you know.

Marti   I know. I'm the two ends of Montgomery Clift, don't tell me.

Marti *and* **George** *exit.* **Dean** *proudly takes off his coat, brushes it down and rests it neatly on the back of the sofa.*

Dean (*to* **Shaun**)   How's life on your own?

Shaun   I'll hang that up for you.

Dean   Oh. Thank you very crutch.

Shaun *hangs* **Dean**'s *coat up on the back of the door.*

Dean   We gonna go out for that drink some time?

Shaun   I don't think so.

Dean   Scared I might pounce?

Shaun   No. (*Returning to seat. To* **Clarine**.) Dean works in McDonald's.

Dean   All work and no play makes Dean a very dull boy. I like playing. Enjoy the odd game.

Shaun   Yeah, and we all know which side you bat for an'all.

Dean   You got a problem with that?

Shaun   I was weaned on queenery.

Dean   Good. What you doing Friday night?

Shaun   Go out with Marti. He thinks you're marvellous.

Dean   I am.

Shaun   Modest an'all.

Dean   I don't blow me own trumpet. Not if I can get someone else to.

Clarine   Do you triple tongue?

Dean   Only the pink oboe. Party on, d'you know what I mean?

Just then **Marti** *shouts from downstairs.*

Marti (*off*)   Shaun?!!

Shaun   What?

Marti (*off*)   Give us an'and wit this!!

Shaun   Scuse me.

Dean   You farted?

Shaun   No.

Clarine *laughs as* **Shaun** *exits. Pause.*

Dean   So. You're a mate o' Shaun's then, yeah?

Clarine   Well, Shaun's my best friend, and Marti's my second best friend, but I don't like George coz she's a slut.

The phone rings.

Clarine   That'll be the phone.

Dean   You get it. Dare ya. It's better when a woman answers the phone.

They both stare at the phone.

Clarine   Oright. (*Picks it up.*) Hello? (*Pause.*) Hiya mam. (*Beat.*) Yeah. (*Beat.*) No. (*Beat.*) Yeah. I know. What's the weather like your end? (*Pause. Then she puts the phone down.*) How did she know I were here?

Dean   Musta tried your number and guessed you was here.

Clarine   But I haven't got a phone.

Shaun *enters followed by* **Marti**, *then* **George** *who is pushing a hostess trolley.*

Shaun   Who was that?

Clarine   Oh, just me mum rang up for a gab. I told her I was at a function.

Shaun   Your mam?!

Marti   How did your mam know you were here?

Clarine   I give her this number. Mmm, something smells nice.

Shaun   Are you sure it was your mam?

Clarine   I know me own mam when I speak to her, thank you, Shaun!

Shaun   But you don't even know who you are!

Dean   Do what?

Clarine   I do. But it's . . . top secret. I haven't to tell a soul!

Shaun   You/what?

Clarine   There's no point rowing with me/Shaun.

Marti   Yeah, come on, Shaun, sit down.

Shaun   Piss off, you, this is my flat.

Marti   And I'm your guardian angel, now park yer arse!

Dean   Hang on a minute . . .

Clarine   Anyway, George, happy birthday.

George (*phased*)   Thanks.

Dean (*to* **George**)   Oh. Happy birthday. Didn't/realise.

Marti   It's nobody's birthday, love. It's a house meal.

Shaun   House meal plus two.

George   I'll serve up, shall I?

As the conversation continues, **George** *ladles up the aubergine bake onto plates and passes them round. They end up eating off their knees.* **Marti** *is sitting in the right-hand chair,* **Shaun** *will be in the left.* **George**, **Clarine** *and* **Dean** *end up sitting on the couch between them.* **Shaun** *is still standing.*

Marti (*to* **Shaun**)   You invited me!

Dean   Don't give you too much heartache to see me, does it, Shaun?

Marti   Actually you didn't invite me, you begged me, now sit down. You've proved your point.

Shaun   Seen Ricky lately, Mart?

Clarine (*plate*)   What are they?

George   Aubergines.

Marti (*to* **Shaun**)   I'd have a job, wouldn't I?

Dean   Is there anything edible in this?

George   All nature's finest.

Dean   What no meat?

George   You remind me of my ex, Malcolm. He was forever bemoaning the state of my meat-free intake. The times he wailed on, 'Meat! Gimme Meat!'

Dean   Like a bit, did he?

George   Adored it.

Clarine   Was he handsome?

George   I thought so. Yes. He was handsome. Would you say he was handsome, Shaun?

Shaun   Who?

George   Malcolm.

Shaun   Beauty's in the eye of the beholder.

Marti   Mm, and some people are bog-eyed.

Shaun   Actually . . .

Marti   Oh, we're getting a lecture here, he used three syllables.

Shaun   I tell yeh who did look like Malcolm.

George   Who?

Shaun   Ricky.

Dean   Who's Ricky then?

Marti   No one.

Shaun   No one? But he was really special to you at one point.

Dean   Was he horny?

George   Well, if he was anything like Malcom he would have been. He was like a heat-seeking baboon.

Dean   Seeing anyone now?

George   No. I really value my independence.

Dean (*to* **Clarine**)   You got anyone?

Clarine Yeah.

George Really? Oh, fantastic. Isn't that great, everybody? Grace has got a beau. Where did you meet him?

Clarine He came visiting the last place I lived.

George Really?

Clarine He said I had nice hair.

George You have got a really fine head of hair on you actually you know, Grace. Don't you think so, Shaun? Sort of . . . Hairdresser Heaven, yeah?

Shaun It's just hair really, isn't it.

George And does he have a name?

Clarine Prince Charles.

Dean What?

Clarine (*sheepish*)   Prince Charles.

Dean Are you taking the piss?

Clarine No.

Shaun Dean.

Dean (*to* **Clarine**)   Are you fucking mental?

Pause.

George I met this guy on a demo on Saturday. Asked for my phone number. On the pretext of sending me some SWP paraphernalia. But I don't know. How about you, Marti?

Marti Sorry?

George Is there a significant other in your life?

Marti I had enough of that in me misspent youth. Two ran off with other women. One joined a monastery. The other had his hair permed. Mortal sin.

Shaun And then of course there was Rich Ricky from Rain Hill. Our Marti, oh, you'll laugh when you hear this. Our Marti had a run of bad luck with fellas.

Marti   How would you know?

Shaun   If they weren't robbing him they were cheating on him. One blew three grand of his savings.

Dean   Who? I'll deck him for ya.

Shaun   And we started thinking. Maybe that's what he attracts. Maybe there's something in Marti that's ... anyway. He proved us all wrong. Where were you at the time?

Marti   I dunno.

Shaun   Glasgow it was. Yeah, out of the blue there's a new man. Ricky. Swimming in money. Made his money in Quorn.

George   Excellent, the vegetarian alternative.

Shaun   Marti was getting whisked off abroad, holidays left, right and centre, we never saw a postcard mind, well, he was too busy having a good time. And did Ricky love him? Did Ricky love him?

Marti   Shaun, please ...

Shaun   Yes. Ricky loved him.

Pause.

Shaun   Well, you can imagine, me mum and dad were dying to meet this Ricky. Pester pester pester. 'When's Ricky coming down?'

Marti   Me dad wasn't arsed, it was me 'arl girl.

Shaun   And as luck would have it Marti and Ricky were doing a whistle-stop tour to the North West. We could have an hour of their time. The big day came. Ricky seemed nervous. Did he seem nervous to you, Marti? Well, he seemed very nervous to me. And Ricky's got this suit on. Next. And unbeknownst to Marti, me mum had had central heating put in. Now she was very proud of her central heating, wasn't she, Marti?

Marti   Social climbing bitch.

Shaun   So in order to show it off, to show he never came from a bad home, she turns it up and makes Ricky take his jacket off.

And in order to show what a good host she was she made me hang it up in the wardrobe upstairs. Now I'm hanging it up and, okay, curiosity got the better of me and I thought . . . I want to see his American Express Gold Card. Coz Marti said he's got one.

George Wow.

Shaun So I have a little look in his inside pocket. No wallet. But I did find . . .

Pause.

A UB40. With the name HUGHIE GRAHAM on it. (*Starts to laugh.*)

George Right.

Dean I don't get it.

Shaun Oh, Dean. Marti had invented Ricky to make out he could manage the perfect relationship.

Marti I never. Ricky . . . Ricky couldn't come at the last minute so I brought me mate Hughie in his place. Well, is there anything wrong in trying to keep your pride?

Shaun Six months later Ricky was killed in an avalanche on a skiing holiday. The family sent Marti cards. (*Beat.*) I never. (*Pause. To* **Marti**.) I had to sit and watch me mother sobbing her heart out coz she was worried sick about how you were taking it.

Marti It near killed me. And you can sit there and joke about it.

A longer silence.

George Has there been anyone since?

Marti I wouldn't trust anyone who said they loved me.

Dean Hey, Marti. Any dirt to dig on Shaun?

George Yes! What don't we know from his sordid past, pre-Juliet?

Dean What was he like at sixteen? Was he a looker?

Pause.

George   Mm?

Marti   I don't know.

Pause. **Dean** *laughs.*

George   You don't know?

Marti   Don't laugh at me.

Shaun   She's not laughing at yeh, Marti.

Dean   No one's laughing at ya.

Clarine   Yes you were.

Marti *gets up and helps himself to a drink.*

Marti   When Shaun. When Shaun found out I was gay . . .

Shaun   Oh, Marti, this is/irrelevant.

Marti   They want to/know.

Shaun   It's totally/irrelevant!

Marti   An eye for an eye, you little twat! When Shaun found out I was gay . . .

George   Look, if this is going to cause/any uneasiness . . .

Marti   You have just asked me a question which I am now going to/answer.

Dean   Watch yourself,/Marti.

Shaun   I think they've probably guessed I didn't take an ad in the *Liverpool Echo* expressing my profound euphoria.

Marti   He threw a spanner at me. He was fixing his moped.

Shaun   It was a scrambler.

Marti   It was a Honda Express. A turquoise Honda Express. He threw a spanner at me . . . and then proceeded to beat ten different types of shite out of me. Sweet sixteen, and I was twenty-six. A toast.

Shaun   You're making a cunt outa yourself.

Marti   To brothers!

Shaun The Honda Express was me mother's. I'd just fixed it for her.

Marti (*a toast*) And to me mother, God love the bones of her!

Shaun The bike I was fixing was my scrambler.

Marti I didn't speak to him for years. Moved around the country. He was still in Liverpool. I'm sure he didn't mean it. Peer pressure (*American.*) and stuff. (*Himself.*) Well, he reckons it was. Fed up of me cajoling him into scenes from *Mildred Pierce, All About Eve* and worse. Well, I was asking for trouble, wasn't I?

Dean All right, Marti, sit down.

Marti I haven't started yet.

Dean Don't work yourself up, man./You're working yourself . . .

Marti (*slapping* **Dean**) Don't call me man!! I fucking hate that! Everyone calls each other MAN now. Even women. It's so fucking/American!

Shaun But yer are a man!

Marti I know what I am. I don't need you spelling it out.

Dean *stands and sits* **Marti** *down.*

Dean Aye aye aye aye, easy, boy.

He sits back down.

Marti So you can imagine how I felt when I bumped into him in a nightclub in Hammersmith two years back. A gay nightclub.

George Right.

Marti He was with her of course. It was then I discovered his political stance had swung somewhat from the right of Adolf Hitler to just a tad to the left of Kenny Livingstone. It was then I was allowed to be his big brother again. I haven't a clue what he was like at sixteen. I was nursing a few wounds in casualty.

Pause.

Clarine Is there any salt?

George   Here.

Shaun   You nasty fucking twat.

Marti   Well, at least we're getting some other emotion from you instead of self-pity. What's the atlas for? So you can trace her route?

Shaun   At least I'm capable of love.

Marti   If that's love, sitting in all day and being a burden to your mates you can stick love.

Shaun   Yeah, well, at least I don't have to go sniffing round some minty fucking piss trough to find it.

Marti   You think I'm looking for love in there? Do yeh? Are you that short-sighted? Get a pair o' glasses, love!

Shaun   Well, what are you looking for? Sympathy? Coz that's the only reason anyone would wanna go near you.

Marti   You'll never understand, will you.

Shaun   Understand what, Mart?

Marti   Me, dear, me.

Pause. The others are eating.

Shaun   Well, who says I'd want to? Who's to say I haven't done all this for her benefit? To prove to Juliet I'm not the bastard I was.

*Pause. No response from **Marti**, it's really winded him. **Shaun** stands.*

Shaun   Fancy that drink, Dean?

Dean (*beat*)   Why not?

Shaun   Come 'ed then. (*To **George**.*) I appreciate what you're doing for me and all that but, you know.

George   That's cool.

Dean (*to **Clarine***)   See you. (*To **Marti**.*) Marti, mate, chill out.

Clarine   Bye. Bye, Shaun.

Shaun   See yeh.

Dean *exits followed by* **Shaun**. **Clarine** *and* **George** *are still eating.* **Marti** *isn't touching his food.*

Marti   Sixteen bruises that lad gave me. One for every year that he hated me. I used to think I was lucky he never had a knife. Well, he's used it now.

George *goes to say something.*

Marti   And if I hear another word out of you about that gobshite Malcolm I'll rip your head off and shit down your neck.

George *says nothing. She is repulsed. She gets up and scrapes her dinner back into the compartment in the hostess trolley.*

George   Think I'll er, catch up on some marking.

George *exits.* **Clarine** *has finished her dinner. She looks at* **Marti**'s *full plate.*

Clarine   Are you gonna eat that? (**Marti** *shrugs.*) Give it here then.

She gets up and takes it off him. She returns to her seat and starts eating it. She smiles at him.

Nice party.

Blackout.

'Big Mouth Strikes Again' by The Smiths plays.

Act Two

Scene One

A week later. Late at night. It's pouring with rain outside. Empty flat. Key in the door. **Dean** *comes in and sits on the bed. He's dressed as himself. Eventually* **Marti** *comes in fumbling in his pocket for a lighter. They're both a bit the worse for wear for drink.* **Marti** *puts the light on. They are both soaked to the skin.* **Marti** *puts the fire on and stands in front of it.*

Marti   D'you want something to put on?

Dean   You're all right.

Marti   You're soaked through.

Marti *goes in the chest of drawers and gets a selection of jogging bottoms and T-shirts which he drapes over the settee. He starts undressing.*

Dean   I can't wear his clothes.

Marti   He won't know. He won't be back for a week.

Dean   Did you see him in Liverpool?

Marti   Didn't hang around.

Dean   I hate Liverpool.

Marti   Been, have yeh?

Dean   What d'you call a Scouser in a suit?

Marti (*offering some jogging bottoms*)   Put these on. You'll catch pneumonia.

Dean   What *do* you call a Scouser in a suit?

Marti   I don't really care.

Dean   I can't wear his clothes. Aint right. Why d'you go back to Liverpool?

Marti   Why shouldn't I go back?

Dean   Guilty. That's what you call 'em. Guilty. What's it like?

Marti   What?

Dean   Liverpool!

Marti   I don't know.

Marti *changes into* **Shaun**'s *dressing-gown off the back of the door. He gets a kimono, Juliet's.*

Marti   D'you want this?

Dean   You walk down a street. Full of robbers and thieves. You get your car nicked, that's why you're walking. You bump into some git who reckons he knew the Beatles. You duff up some other git coz he aint got a Liverpool accent then you have a ride on the ferry. That's what it's like. That plant don't look too healthy.

Marti   Shit.

Marti *goes out to the landing.* **Dean** *gets undressed, apart from his jeans, and puts on Juliet's kimono.* **Marti** *returns with a kebab.*

Marti   Left it in the bog.

Dean   You wanna move that plant.

Marti   Do I?

Dean   It's too near the radiator. That's why it's dry.

Marti   You wanna go to Liverpool. Find out what it's really like.

Dean   I don't think I could compete with your salt-of-the-earth humour.

Marti   Ooh, you reckon you know it all you Southerners. Everyone's got a take on Liverpool, but nobody's really been.

Dean   This isn't casual by the way.

Marti   Since when were you green-fingered?

Dean   I water all the plants at work.

Dean *kicks his shoes off.* **Marti** *sits on the couch eating his kebab.*

Dean   I gotta say it.

Marti   Liverpool is the pool of life. That's what it means.

Dean   I've never touched you before.

Marti   You could have done in the club. You can't tell one from the other with the lights off.

Dean   I can.

Marti   (*kebab*)   D'you want any o' this?

Dean   Marti. That short for Martin? I can't think of you as a Martin.

Marti   David.

Dean   David?

Marti   Me second name's Caine. They used to call our Shaun Michael and me . . .

Dean   Marti. Caine.

Marti   It stuck.

Dean   He was really cut up when we went for that drink.

Marti   Was he?

Dean   No. But I reckon he was underneath it all.

Marti   I thought you fancied our Shaun?

Dean   I was just using him to get to you.

Marti   Piss off.

Dean   You shouldn't wear black, don't suit ya.

Marti   Did you know they make kebab meat out of crushed bones?

Dean   So?

Marti   You didn't, did you? He told me that.

Pause.

I'm not wearing black.

Dean   It just come to me.

Marti   Why shouldn't I?

Dean   Blue's your colour.

Pause.

Funny things, beds.

Marti   No, they're not.

Dean   You sleep in them. You shag in them. And you make love in them.

Marti   So there's a distinction is there?

Dean   I'm through with it all, Marti, messing around.

Pause.

Come here.

Pause. **Marti** *goes and looks out of the window, eating his kebab.*

Marti.

Marti   It's pissing down.

Dean   I know.

Pause.

Marti   I'm not very good at sex these days.

Dean   Fair enough, we won't have sex.

Marti   It's too messy. I don't like things that put me in touch with me own mortality.

Dean   You do in the dark room.

Marti   When I'm off me face.

Pause.

I wish it was different. I wish I was. When you're a teenager you try to be someone else. You spend your twenties discovering who you really are. And you spend your thirties getting used to it.

Dean   I love you, man.

Marti   No, you don't.

Dean   You love me. You do, you told me the other week.

Marti   When?

Dean   In the club. No, not in the club. After, in the cab. You held my hand all the way home and you told me you loved me.

Marti   I was off me face.

Dean *peels off his kimono. He stands there in his wet jeans and white vest starting at* **Marti**.

Marti   Oh, Dean. You're a sweet boy.

Dean   You gotta open yourself up to being loved.

Marti   I only fall in love with people I can never have. It's easier like that.

Dean   Why?

Marti   Less mess.

Dean *goes and switches the light off. They're now in total darkness.*

Dean   Does this help?

Marti *steps forwards and walks into the settee. He spills his kebab on it.*

Marti   Oh, fuckinell, switch it back on.

Dean *switches the light back on. We see the spilt kebab.*

Marti   Oh, God. I asked for extra chilli sauce.

Dean   Don't matter.

Marti   I can wash it.

Dean   Not now.

Marti   I know.

He goes and sits on the edge of the bed.

Is this some sort of fantasy of yours?

Dean   No.

Marti   Is it coz you've had a few?

Dean   No. I'm serious.

Marti   Make it just a fantasy.

Pause. Then **Dean** *switches the light off again. He unzips his jeans.*

Marti   What's that smell?

Dean   Fahrenheit. Go on.

Marti   Oh, all right. Come over here.

Dean *moves over and stands before* **Marti**.

Marti   Your jeans are wet.

Dean   I know. It's raining. Go on.

Marti   Where is it?

Dean   Here.

Marti   Eh?

Dean's *fly goes up. He puts the light back on.* **Marti**'s *sitting on the bed.* **Dean** *doesn't know where to put himself.*

Marti   Do it again and keep the lights on.

Dean   S'all right.

Marti   I don't mind.

Dean   Nah, s'all right.

Marti   Honestly.

Dean   Gotta get back. Gotta feed my snake.

He starts putting his wet clothes on.

Marti   You're gonna catch pneumonia.

Dean   I'm all right.

Marti   Stay.

Dean   I can't.

Marti   Dean.

Dean   What?

Marti   I prefer it when you're Fifi Trixabelle La Bouche.

Dean *finishes dressing.*

Marti   Go and feed your snake eh?

Dean   Later, Mart.

Marti   Yeah.

As **Dean** *exits.* **George** *enters with a bottle of red wine and two glasses. She sort of bumps into him.*

George   Oh, sorry.

Dean *exits with no comment.*

George   I'm sorry. I heard footsteps. I thought Shaun was away.

Marti   He is.

George   Thought he'd made an early return.

Marti   No.

George   Right. I'll. Sorry.

Marti   He should be back by the end of the week.

George   Don't suppose you fancy a nightcap? I tried Grace but I couldn't get much sense out of her. Something about rats.

Marti   Go on then.

George   No, if ...

Marti   No, it's ...

George   Well, if you're sure.

She sits on the sofa and pours two glasses of wine. **Marti** *sits in the right armchair.*

George   Shaun did say *you* were in Liverpool.

Marti   The place we go to lick our wounds.

George   Did you get bored?

Marti   He turned up to lick his, so I come back down.

George   Here. (*She hands him a glass.*)

Marti   Tar.

George   Cheers.

Marti   Probably just what he needs, the home comforts.

George   We can all do with those every now and again.

Marti   I was out round here tonight so I thought I'd stay over. I'd er, appreciate it if you, er, if you didn't tell him you seen me. If you didn't tell him I'd been.

George   If I don't that kebab will.

Marti   I'll wash it.

George   It's a bit odd, him going home. I'd have thought he'd want to look after the business.

Marti   I know. There's scores of grannies all over London whose blue rinses are fading away. What will they do without Curls on Wheels?

George   Find another stylist if they've got any sense.

Marti   But do I care?

George   Yes. I think you do.

Marti   Juliet'll kill him if she gets back and the business is rotten.

George   Do you think things are hunky-dory between them?

Marti   Don't you?

George   Well, four weeks seems an awfully long time to be away for a funeral.

Marti   Well, Christ, girl, if you had the choice between a sunny beach and Bromley-by-Bow, which would you choose?

George   True. I'm going camping next week.

Marti   Camp.

George   Daffyd's invited me.

Marti   Daffyd?

George   A certain knight in shining armour with the biggest SWP placard I've held in months.

Marti   Christ, George!! You didn't waste any time, did yeh?

George   It's not as romantic as it sounds. Though how wading through a muddy field in the Forest of Dean could ever be termed romantic is beyond me. No. He was already going with some SWP chums and he asked if I wanted to tag along. It's half-term next week, so.

Marti   You're grabbing life by the short and curlies.

George   Well, I'll have my own tent. Oh, I'm so looking forward to it, you know, Marti. Though I'll have bundles of moderating to plough through. We're reaching that time of the year where GCSE bells start ringing through the air.

Shaun *has entered during this last speech. He's soaked to the skin and carrying a sports bag. Pause. He stands there.*

Shaun   All right?

Marti   I was out with Dean. Couldn't get a cab.

Shaun   I've always said you could stay. I give you a key, didn't I?

Shaun *starts unpacking his sports bag on the bed.*

Marti   George heard me in here and thought you were back.

George   Glass of wine?

Shaun   No, tar.

Marti   It's got a lovely bouquet.

Shaun   You're all right.

George   I better go downstairs.

Marti   Right.

George (*to* **Marti**)   Finish this off. (*Leaves bottle.*)

Marti   Oh, tar. Night, love. Enjoy your tent.

George   Night, Shaun.

Shaun   Night.

George (*to* **Marti**)   Night.

George *exits, taking her glass of wine with her.* **Shaun** *still unpacking his bag.* **Marti** *gets up and starts tidying away the selection of jogging bottoms off the couch.*

Marti You should put something else on. You'll catch your death.

Shaun   I'll just finish this.

Marti How's mum?

Shaun   Fine.

Marti Dad?

Shaun   Same as when you left 'em.

Marti Look, I'll get out from under your feet . . .

Pause.

Shaun   Marti.

Marti Mm?

Shaun   You don't have to get off.

Marti No, I know what it's like when you wanna get a bit o' peace and quiet.

Shaun   Marti, why d'you think I went to Liverpool?

Marti Homesick?

Shaun   I went to talk to you. Oh, listen I will have that drink.

Marti I'll get yer a glass.

Shaun   Okay.

Marti *goes off to kitchen.* **Shaun** *gets a present out of the bag. It's a video in an Our Price bag. He puts it on the coffee-table. He removes the kebab from the couch and puts it in the bin. He starts stripping the stretch cover off the couch.* **Marti** *returns with a glass.*

Marti Oh, I'm sorry about that.

Shaun   It's all right.

Marti I was gonna wash it in the morning.

Shaun   I'll stick it in to soak overnight.

Shaun *exits to kitchen with the cover. We hear him running the taps to soak the cover.*

Marti   It's about time you washed it. I'm surprised it can't stand up on it's own.

Shaun (*off*)   I decided I'd do a big spring-clean as soon as I'd heard from Juliet.

Marti   Oh, right.

Shaun (*off*)   Better start tomorrow.

Marti   Did she ring?

Shaun (*off*)   I rang her. Me ma was going spare. 'You ringing that Barbados again?' I wasn't on for long. She said she'd sent us a letter so it should be here any day now.

Marti   Hence your early return.

Shaun (*coming back in*)   Curls on Wheels won't run itself. I made a few appointments while I was up there. I'm doing an old people's home in Greenwich all day tomorrow.

Marti   It's all go in the world of perming.

Shaun   And . . . I wanted to give you this.

Shaun *hands* **Marti** *the video in the bag.* **Marti** *gets it out.*

Marti   Oh, fabulous! The Nanny!

Shaun   Bette Davis.

Marti   Oh, Shaun.

Shaun   Thought it might give yer a few more lines.

Marti   On me face?

Shaun   To speak. I asked if they'd got anything with Joan Crawford in as well but . . .

Marti   Any fool knows they only did *Baby Jane* together.

Shaun   I forgot. The fella in Our Price gave me daggers when I asked. I think he might've been a queen.

Marti   Well, they were slated to do *Hush . . . Hush, Sweet Charlotte* together but Crawford did a few scenes then backed out, the bitch.

Shaun   I'm sorry, Marti.

Marti   I hate falling out with people. I don't wanna go
through life not being able to speak to the people I care about.
Whenever I meet someone new, or someone who shows an
interest, mates, you know, not lovers or anything, I'm always full
of this foreboding. It's like, I can't trust anything. It's like I'm
waiting for them to catch me out. I'm always expecting things to
go wrong. And then they do, they always do. I dunno, maybe me
moon's in Uranus or something. Some bad planets colliding up
there. That's how it feels at the moment.

Shaun   It won't last forever.

Marti   I hope you're right. I really do.

Shaun   You create your own reality.

Marti   Where d'you learn that? Back of a cornflakes packet?

Shaun (*shakes head*)   Off the woman I love. The woman I'm
gonna keep. And from now on I'm gonna start acting like I
deserve her and get me act together.

Marti   Positive thinking? I've heard about that, but I'm
always too miserable to try it.

Shaun (*toast*)   To the future, kid.

Marti   You've changed your tune.

Shaun   Well, it was about time. Now stick that tape on.

Marti   Now?

Shaun *nods*. **Marti** *gets the tape out and puts it in the video.* **Shaun**
*switches the light off and slips out of his wet clothes. He sticks some jogging
bottoms on and a sweatshirt. They are lit now from the light from the screen.*

Shaun   D'you wanna stay with me till Juliet gets back?

Marti (*nods*)   All right. If you want.

Shaun   I'll cook us something nice for our tea tomorrow.

Marti   You're still quite new to me.

Pause.

Well, it worries me.

Shaun   Fast forward through this bit.

Marti *sits on the sofa with the remote control and fast forwards the video. He has a look at the cover and reads the blurb on the back.*

Marti (*reading*)   'The Fane family trusted Nanny, she helped them cope with the sudden death of their baby daughter. Young Joey didn't.'

Shaun   Wise man!

Marti   'He knew Nanny would do anything to remain Head of the Household. When the key suspects of murder are narrowed down to Nanny and the disturbed youngster, a frightening chain of events begins. Starring Bette Davis and Wendy Craig!'

They laugh. **Marti** *fires the remote at the telly. The video begins.* **Shaun** *has got changed and sits down in the right armchair. They are laughing. As the lights fade 'The Sunshine After The Rain' by Berri plays, leading us into the next scene.*

Scene Two

Marti'*s in on his own, chopping up a pineapple on the coffee-table. Berri is playing loudly on the stereo, and* **Marti** *is singing along to it. A clean stretch cover graces the couch. There is a knock at the door. He turns the volume down and opens the door to* **Clarine**. *She is wearing a T-shirt with the logo 'Barbados' on it. She is still speaking with a Rochdale accent.*

Clarine   Hiya.

Marti   Hiya, doll, is me music too loud?

Clarine   No, it's the rats.

Marti   You haven't got rats.

Clarine (*nods*)   Hoards of 'em.

Marti   Oh, God, you wanna get onto the council about that.

Clarine   I already have. They're sending someone round. (*Beat.*) Fruit salad. Very nice. Where's Shaun?

Marti   Just popped the shop for a tub o'yoghurt. He's making a curry in there.

Clarine   I like Shaun. He looks like Adam Faith, out of *Love Hurts*.

Marti (*laughs*)   I didn't know you'd been to Barbados.

Clarine   That's coz I haven't.

Marti   Well, where d'you get the top?

Clarine   Me mam give it me.

Marti   Has she been?

Clarine   Here?

Marti   Barbados.

Clarine   No. I don't think so, why?

Marti   Well, coz o' your top.

Clarine   Is that what it says?

Marti   Yeah.

Clarine   Barbados.

Pause. **Marti** *carries on chopping the pineapple.* **Clarine** *looks at her T-shirt, then puts a cushion on her knee to cover it up.*

Clarine   I'm on me period.

Marti   Goway.

Shaun *enters with shopping.*

Shaun   Hiya.

Clarine   Hiya, I'm on me period.

Shaun   Yeah?

Clarine   I've got tights on though.

Marti   Oh, well, you're laughing then.

Clarine   I've always liked tights.

Shaun (*handing money to* **Marti**)   Here's your change. (*To* **Clarine**.) Can I get yer a coffee?

Clarine   No, I might have an accident.

Marti (*to* **Shaun**)   Tar.

Clarine (*to* **Marti**)   I like you living here.

Shaun *goes into kitchen.*

Marti   Well, it's not for long so make the most o'me. Then you'll meet Juliet.

Clarine   Is she pretty?

Marti   Juliet? She's gorgeous.

Shaun *comes to the kitchen door.*

Marti   She used to be a model but she helps Shaun out with the hairdressing now. They met at a hairdressing competition.

Clarine   Has she got lovely long blonde hair and blue eyes and legs that go on forever?

Shaun   No, she's mixed race.

Clarine   I was in a mixed race once.

Shaun   No. She's black.

Marti   As in the colour of skin.

Shaun   Her mum was white and her dad was black.

Marti   So that makes her mixed race.

Clarine   Egg and spoon.

Marti   But she's got too much up top to be a model. She's the brains of the business.

Shaun   Oh aye?

Clarine   They played a joke on me. Everyone else's was hard-boiled and mine was raw. Stacey McNamara tripped me up halfway and I got yolk down me nylons.

Pause.

Marti   She reckons she's got rats.

Shaun   Have yeh?

Clarine   Mm.

Marti   Have you seen these rats?

Clarine   I've heard them. Calling me names.

Shaun   I'm not being funny wit yer, Clarine, but, rats can't speak.

Clarine   These are a special breed. Don't call me Clarine. I don't call you Norman. They tell me to do things.

Marti   Have you got any tablets you should be taking?

Clarine   Can we have another party? I liked the last one.

Shaun   When Juliet gets back. We'll have one then. A big one. Coz she'll want to see all her mates.

Clarine *puts the cushion down, excited.*

Clarine   You'll want to have a party when you hear me news.

Shaun   Barbados?

Clarine   Yeah, it's nice, int it? Me mam gave me this.

Shaun   Has she been?

Clarine   Yeah.

Shaun   Goway. D'you wanna brew, Mart?

Marti   No thanks.

Shaun *exits to kitchen.*

Marti   If you wanna stay for something to eat, you know, Clarine, you're more than welcome.

Clarine   Sharon.

Marti   You what?

Clarine   That's me news. Today. I remembered me name.

Marti   Ah, excellent!

Clarine   Tar.

Marti   How did you remember?

Clarine   A leaflet came. And I read it. And it said Sharon. And that's when I remembered. And I asked someone in the launderette what the map on it was. And they said it was directions to the sorting office. So I went and handed the leaflet in and they gave me a parcel.

Marti   Who was it from?

Clarine   Me mam. But. Me mam's dead.

Pause.

Marti   What was in it?

Clarine   A T-shirt, a box of chocolates, two pairs of underpants, a photo of this girl, and a letter. But I couldn't read all of it, but I don't care coz it reminded me what my name is. Sharon.

Marti   Right. Oh, well, that's brilliant. Ah, I'm made up for you!

Shaun *appears at the door of the kitchen holding a photo.*

Shaun   Was this the girl?

Clarine   Eh?

Shaun   The photo in the parcel. Was that her?

He hands **Clarine** *the photo.*

Shaun   Well?

Marti   Shaun?

Shaun   Barbados?! Are you as daft as her?

Marti   Shaun!!

Shaun   Shaun. Sharon. Sharon. Shaun. She can't read!

Clarine   I can read me own name.

Shaun   Where's this parcel? What've you done with it? Go and get it now!

Clarine   I can't.

Shaun   Just do it!

Clarine   I threw it away. I don't want underpants.

Shaun   Listen titforbrains, my bird is in Barbados. She said she'd sent us something. Now go and find it.

Clarine   Bin men have been.

Shaun   Y'what?!

Clarine   Eh?

Marti   Well, did you keep the letter?

Clarine   I don't know.

Shaun   Oh, I don't fucking believe this!

Marti   Calm down, softtwat. Clarine. Sharon. Come upstairs wit me and we'll see if we can find anything.

Clarine   It was from me mam, I know it was!

Shaun   But you've just said your mam's dead!

Clarine   Yeah, well, she could've sent it before she died or anything, couldn't she? Yeah!

Shaun   You've only lived here for three weeks. How did she know your address!

Clarine   It was for me. I know it was for me.

Marti   Sharon, love, come on.

Shaun   Sharon. Look at this girl here. (*Photo.*) You've seen her before, haven't you?

Clarine   Yeah.

Shaun   Thank you.

Clarine   That's me mam that.

Shaun *is deflated.*

Marti   Come on, love. We're going upstairs.

Clarine   I'm not daft.

Clarine *exits.*

Marti   Shaun, she can't help herself.

Shaun   She can help herself to my property.

Marti   She's sick, Shaun.

Shaun   Well, so am I.

Marti *goes after* **Clarine**. *Left alone,* **Shaun** *dives for the phone and dials the international number again.*

Shaun   Hello? Hello can I speak to Juliet please? (*Beat.*) Isn't she? (*Beat.*) Can you tell her Shaun rang? (*Pause.*) Have you got a number for there? (*Beat.*) Hello? (*Beat.*) Hello?

He puts the phone down. Immediately it rings again. He snaps it up.

Shaun   Hello? (*Pause.*) No she's away at the moment. She'll be back in two weeks. Who's this? (*Pause.*) Andy? (*Pause.*) Shaun. I'm her boyfriend. (*Pause.*) Hello? Hello?

Marti *has entered. He holds a chocolate box.* **Shaun** *takes it and opens it. It is empty. He shakes it upside-down to show* **Marti**.

Shaun   The greedy bitch!

Marti   She said she didn't eat them.

Shaun   And who did? A gang of Oxford don rats?

Marti   Well, yeah, actually. (*Takes the box off him and puts it on the table*.) She'll balloon.

Shaun   Why chocolates? We're supposed to be vegan. (*Cries.*)

Marti   Oh, Shaun, what happened to all this positive thinking?

Shaun   You know how much that letter means to me.

Marti   Okay, okay.

Shaun   I've spoken to her *once* since she's been away. I've just had some fella ringing up for her. I get one letter off her and *she's* fucking gone and nicked it on me. I hate living here.

Marti   Oh, now stop it. Stop it! She's crying. You're crying. Maybe I feel like crying an' all.

Shaun   I'm going up to look. You weren't up there long, you mighta missed something.

Marti   Shaun, she's got nothing in that flat bar a bare table, a mattress and a guitar. If she'd dropped a contact lens I'da been able to see it.

Shaun   Well, where are her clothes? She must have clothes.

Marti   Okay, there's a pile of dirty washing as well. Shaun, I want you to have Juliet's letter as much as you do. I looked.

Shaun   I'm gonna ring someone about that girl.

Marti   Well, try Virginia Bottomley for starters.

Shaun   Oh, you've got to bring politics into everything you.

Marti   Right, that's it. I'm phoning a cab. It's pointless me being here. I've got a nice easy flat in Stoke Newington. Nice neighbours. Artists, couriers. I can do without this.

Shaun   Someone wants to pull her up. You're not telling me she can get away with this. You don't seriously believe that, do yeh?

Marti   There's a pineapple, there's your knife. Sculpt it into the face of Juliet and give us all a break. (*Picks phone up. Dials a local number.*)

Shaun   Oh, you can't run out on me now.

Marti (*on phone*)   Can I have a cab, please? Yeah. 15 Rupert Street . . .

Shaun *cuts him off by slamming his hand on the phone.*

Marti   Well, that was rather childish, wasn't it?

Shaun *has frozen.* **Marti** *drops the phone and goes to the kitchen.*

Shaun   What you doing?

Marti   Checking the vindaloo! (*Exits.*)

Shaun, *left alone, kicks the couch. He chucks a cushion off it across the room. He looks for something else to throw. He gets the pineapple and hurls that backstage as well.* **Marti** *returns as he does this. He goes and retrieves the pineapple and then heads back to the kitchen again.* **Shaun** *sits down fuming. A tap runs in the kitchen, then is switched off.* **Marti** *returns with the pineapple and carries on preparing the fruit salad.* **Shaun** *lies on the bed and puts a pillow over his head.*

Marti   If you're tryina do an impersonation of me gran you're gonna need a rope and a chair. You tie the noose. I'll kick the chair away for yeh.

Shaun *hurls the pillow at* **Marti**. *He catches it.*

Marti   Can't you phone Juliet?

Shaun   She's not in, is she. She's gone to a barbecue.

Marti   Well, she'll be having a ball then. Can't you just enjoy the idea of that?

Shaun   What's she gonna eat at a barbie? She's vegan!

Marti   Well, don't they have Linda McCartney sausages out there?

Pause. Disheartened, **Marti** *throws his knife down on the coffee-table and buries his head in his hands. He looks up.*

Marti   It's been a crap life this. Maybe next time I'll come back as a prisoner of war. There's bound to be more laughs then. I want the class and campery of a Bette Davis movie and I feel like I'm stuck in an episode of *EastEnders*. Misery, misery, always misery. There's no let up. It's not easy oppression. I'm oppressed, you know.

Shaun   I'm depressed.

Marti   Yeah, well, I'm oppressed and depressed so there. And I'm recessed. And processed. And Beau Jeste. (**Shaun** *stifles a giggle*.) It's no laughing matter. Don't laugh at me, I'm a fool.

Shaun   You're no fool, Marti.

Marti   There's no fool like an old fool.

Shaun   You're not old though.

Marti   I'm thirty-three and I've finally come to realise what I am.

Shaun (*doing his 'Veda' from* Mildred Pierce)   A common frump whose father lived above a grocery store and whose mother . . .

Marti   A coward.

Shaun   Nah. I'm the coward. I'm the one who can't function just coz me bird's away.

Marti   I've spent a lifetime being defensive, being loud, camping it up. It's all armour. To cover up the real coward within.

Shaun   Noël Coward?

Marti   I'm being serious. Why is it the only time I'm not afraid is when I'm three Es under? I am. I'm a coward.

Shaun   Well, the right man comes along.

Marti   Don't you patronise me.

Shaun   I'm not. The right girl came along for me.

Marti   And what if he already did? And I was too scared to say Yes?

Shaun   He'll come back.

Marti   Yeah and he won't find me coz I'm always round here.

Shaun   Phone a cab then.

Marti   Have you seen what's on the telly tonight? *Stolen Life*. The man of my dreams would be a real Bette Davis freak. He's not gonna leave his house while that's on. And neither am I.

Shaun   I remember when I first looked at this ceiling like this. Thought I'd found me own little corner of Paradise. (*Sits up.*) What's *Stolen Life* like?

Marti (*nearly reaching orgasm*)   Bette Davis playing *twins*.

Shaun   We could go for a bevvy after.

Marti   I feel a mess today.

Shaun   Bollocks, you'll have loads of people coming up to yeh.

Marti   And saying 'Who's your mate?' Oh, why can't someone just walk through that door who's got half a brain and thinks Bette Davis is the best thing since sliced bread?

Clarine *enters with a piece of paper.*

Clarine   I've found it.

Pause.

It wasn't from her.

Shaun   What?

Clarine   It was from me mam.

Shaun   Let's see.

Clarine *hands* **Shaun** *the letter. He inspects it.*

Clarine (*sings*)   Every time we say goodbye
I cry a little.
Every time we say goodbye
I wonder why a little.
Why the Gods above me
Who must be in the know
Think so little of me
You decided to go.
I can hear a lark somewhere.

She stops.

(*Speaks.*)   My boyfriend's away at the moment. I understand.

Marti   Shaun didn't mean to shout at you, did you, Shaun?

Clarine   He shouts. He's in Northern Ireland. Visiting the troops. (*Beat.*) I'm stupid you know.

Shaun   No, you're not.

Clarine   I am. All that time forgetting me name.

Marti   It's easily done.

Clarine   It was on me UB40 all the time. Night.

Shaun   Night, Sharon.

She exits. She stands out on the landing. They are unaware that she's still there.

Marti   It's pathetic. She needs to be somewhere where people are going to say Yes, you are stupid. Your behaviour is seriously dodgy. Get a life. Remember who you really are.

Clarine *exits from view.*

Marti   We could all do with a bit of that. I better check that curry hasn't evaporated. What's it say?

Shaun   You're right, Marti. It is pathetic. (*Reads.*) Sharon. Squiggle squiggle squiggle. Mum. Kiss.

Marti *exits to the kitchen.* **Shaun** *looks at the letter. The lights fade. 'Every Time We Say Goodbye' plays, starting at the line 'I can hear a lark somewhere'.*

Scene Three

Later that night. **Marti** *and* **Dean** *enter supporting a very pissed* **Shaun**. **Shaun** *is singing 'American Pie'. Steeleye Span is floating up from downstairs.*

Shaun   (*sings*)   Did you write the book of love?

Dean   Come on.

Shaun   And do you have faith in God above?

Marti   Shaun!

Shaun   If the Bible tells you so.

Marti   D'you want your bed?

Shaun   And do you believe in rock and roll
Can music save your mortal soul
And can you teach me how to dance real slow?

Marti (*to* **Dean**)   Oh, fuck him.

Marti *and* **Dean** *let go of* **Shaun** *and sit down.*

Shaun   Well, I knew you were in love with him
Coz I saw you dancing in the gym.

Marti   He's unrepentedly straight.

Shaun   You both kicked off your shoes
And I did those rhythm and blues.

Marti   Isn't this where we do a counter-attack of 'I Will Survive'?

Shaun *jumps on the bed and keeps on singing.* **Dean** *and* **Marti** *light up some fags.* **Marti** *goes towards the kitchen.*

Marti (*to* **Shaun**)   You're not impressing anyone! (*Exits.*)

Shaun   I was a lonely teenage bronkin' buck
With a pink carnation and a pick-up truck
But I knew that I was out of luck
The day the music died.
I started singing . . .

Dean (*joins in*)   Bye bye Miss American Pie
Drove my chevvy to the levy but the levy
was dry.

Marti (*entering with three cans of lager and joining in*)
Them good old boys were drinking
whisky and rye
Singing this'll be the day that I die.
This'll be the day that I die.

Marti *hands out the three cans, one each.*

Shaun (*speaks*)   You think all the good songs are fucking
'Secret Love' and torch songs and queer anthems. But everyone.
Everyone knows 'American Pie'.

Marti   We haven't all got it in for heterosexuals, you know.

Dean   Both my parents were.

Marti   And mine.

Dean   It's a conspiracy.

Shaun   D'you know what it is? Eh? D'you wanna know what it really is?

Shaun *huddles them together, one either side.*

Shaun   It's . . . bollocks. (*Laughs heartily. Steps back from the huddle.*) Ah Dean lad, d'you know him? (*Puts arm round* **Marti**.) I love this man. And d'you know what? I fucking think the world of him. You know when that Polish cunt fucked him around. I was fucking spitting blood. Ah, I was though. No one. No one messes my brother around. Ah, I was fuming, Marti. I really was. (*Falls onto bed backwards by accident. Not onto his back, but sitting. To* **Dean**.) D'you know what I mean, lad?

Marti (*to* **Dean**)   He's talking to you.

Shaun   Dean. D'you know what I'm saying?

Dean   Yeah, mate.

Shaun *is trying unsuccessfully to get his trainers off.* **Marti** *goes and helps him.*

Marti   I think it was that last tequila slammer that did it.

Shaun   Ah, man. How many tequila slammers did we have?

Dean   I've got some whizz somewhere.

Shaun   About eight?

Dean   Wannabit?

Marti   I love it when I bump into you, Dean, you can always be sure of a wild time.

Shaun   Marti, Marti. (*American.*) You bought the new girdles a size smaller I can feel it.

Dean   Shaun?

Shaun   Something maybe grew a size . . . what?

Marti   He's asking if you want some speed.

Shaun (*dismissive wave of hand, carries on with* All About Eve)   When I get home I'm gonna . . . Marti!!

Marti   I'm having this, aren't I?

Marti *has some of the speed* **Dean** *has passed him.*

Shaun   Ah, well, fuck yeh then yeh bore.

Dean (*to* **Shaun**)   Sure you don't want none?

Shaun   I'm working in the morning.

Marti   You, y'drunken lush, are gonna have a hangover on you the size o' my nobbage in the morning. I don't see how a little bit o' whizz is gonna make much difference.

Dean   Come on. Or are all straight bastards wimps?

Dean *dabs the speed round his gums.*

Shaun   Have you seen *Reservoir Dogs*, Dean?

Dean   Yeah.

Shaun   Have yeh? It's brilliant, isn't it?

Dean   Yeah.

Shaun   It's fucking excellent.

Dean (*about the speed*)   Shame it's not coke.

Marti   Coke on the dole this.

Dean   My snake's called Charlie.

Shaun   Well, give it here then.

Dean   I won't be able to get it up now. (*Passes* **Shaun** *the speed.*)

Marti   Good.

Dean   Listen.

Marti   What?

Dean   Downstairs. That music.

Marti   God, it's loud enough, isn't it?

Shaun *is up off the bed, doing kung fu-ish kick-boxing around the room and talking to himself in an American Deputy Dawg voice.*

Shaun   It's good shit, man! It's good shit!

Shaun *takes a run at the bed, jumps on it like he's in a kung fu film and going in for the kill. He lands and lies on his back and goes to sleep.*

Dean   You're my mate. You know that, dontcha?

Marti   I know.

Dean   Yeah. Mate.

Marti   Good. That's really good that. I do love you, Dean. As that old adage goes.

Dean   I love you, mate. In a friendship way.

Marti   I know.

Dean   It's true, isn't it?

Marti   What?

Dean   Everything.

Marti   Right from the word go. Right from the moment you jammed your stiletto heel through the wire mesh up the top o'the bogs and broke that bulb.

Dean   Life's a train. And we're on that train. And some days it goes real fast right, and some days it goes real . . . slow. Yeah?

Marti   Yeah, like some days you can have a real Orient Express of a day, and the next your riding Ivor the Engine.

Dean   Ah, brilliant, what was the tune?

Marti   I forget.

Dean   Bang-on tune.

Marti   I know, yeah.

Dean   I'm surprised it weren't released on CD.

Marti   Maybe we should.

Dean   Ah, man! We would make seriously big money. Party on, d'you know what I mean?

There is a knock at the door. **Marti** *gets up.*

Marti   I know, yeah.

Dean   Yeah!

Marti *opens the door to* **George** *who holds a glass of red wine. She is wearing jeans and a waistcoat. No shoes.*

George   I heard you coming in. He's downstairs.

Marti   Is he?

George   Yeah.

Marti   Fab. Who?

George   Daffyd!! Had him over for dinner. He's staying over. Insisting I have the futon if you please.

Dean   I do, please. Half of Ilford can't be wrong.

George (*looking at* **Shaun**)   How *is* he?

Marti   He's asleep, God love him.

George   Did you take him out to drown his sorrows?

Marti   He had a bit of speed then fell straight asleep.

George   Juliet wrote and told me. I don't know what to say.

Marti   Told you what?

George   It's so sad, isn't it?

Marti   What?

George   That she'd written to him and done the evil deed. Did she use those words? Sorry, I've had two glasses of wine. Sounds so cold. Evil deed. I don't really believe anybody's evil. How did he take it?

Pause.

George   I know she's a great friend of mine, and I'm not being biased. But I don't think she's evil, do you? You know she doesn't hate him. You know that, don't you? You know at one stage she downright worshipped the guy. Yeah? I'll show you the letter. Don't go away.

She goes to the door and shouts down the stairs.

George   Daffyd! Daffyd!! (*Turns back to* **Marti**.) He's a real Steeleye Span freak. (*Calls.*) Daffyd! Could you get me the letter that's in the pocket of my Gloria Vanderbilt jeans?!! (*Realises she's wearing them.*) Oh, scrap that! I've got them on!

She comes back into the room. She gets a letter out of her pocket. She reads a bit.

George (*reading*)   You probably already know by now, but I've finished with Shaun. It was a cowardly thing to do, I know, telling him by post. But it was the only way.

Marti *sits on the bed.*

George   Sorry. Haven't got my specs on.

Dean *gets up and takes the letter off her. He sits back down and reads.*

Dean   'He was stiffing me. Sorry, stifling. He was stifling me in the end and coming out here I felt such a release. Marti always said he was my bit of rough Scouse trade. Marti's more perceptive than he lets on. Sorry, Marti's Shaun's brother. A real case. Anyway, I hope Shaun's new single lifestyle doesn't cause you too much grief. If he plays his music too loud just give him a knock. He can be quite thoughtful when he's told to be. I just got sick of telling him. I've just read the new Jackie Collins. *Hollywood Kids*.'

Pause.

George   They seemed so good together. Anyway, Daffyd's simmering on a low light down there. It's about time I went in and really started cooking with gas.

Marti   He doesn't know, George, he never got the letter.

George   Shit me.

Dean (*to* **Marti**)   You gotta tell him.

Marti (*to* **George**)   You're Juliet's mate. You've got to tell him.

George   I'm up at seven to go to the Forest of Dean.

Dean   I haven't got a forest.

Marti   Oh, shut up, Dean.

Dean   Sorry, mate.

George   I'm truly sorry.

George *exits*.

Dean   Shit.

Pause.

What you gonna do?

Marti *jumps up, pulls the phone out of the wall then starts attacking the sofa. He claws at it with his hands and kicks it.* **Dean** *gets up to stop him. He pulls him off.* **Marti** *wrestles away and attacks it again.*

Dean   Oi! Oi!

Dean *holds onto him.* **Marti** *pushes him off.* **Marti** *heads for the door.*

Dean   Oi, where d'you think you're going?

Marti   For a walk!

Dean   Hang on.

Marti *exits.* **Dean** *follows with their two coats.* **Shaun** *is left alone in the room, lying on the bed. There is some sort of noise coming out of him, an animal-like groaning. It grows louder. He sits up. He moves over to the letter which* **Dean** *has left on the arm of the chair. He stands reading it. He breathes deeply through his nose. He finishes it. He doesn't cry. He moves over to the stereo. Very calmly he looks through some tapes. He selects one, puts it in the machine and rewinds it. He plays it. It is 'American Pie' by Don McClean. He kneels in front of the stereo and sings along, quietly at first, but getting louder. As he kneels, he folds the letter into an aeroplane shape. He stands up and starts to dance, the letter in his hand. He gets his lager and dances over to the window. He takes a big swig of his lager and opens the window. He throws the letter out of the window. He leaves the window open and goes and turns the music up full-blast. He dances round the room drinking and singing along with the song.*

Clarine *enters in bra and slip. She speaks with a Kidderminster accent.*

Clarine   Turn it down! It's too loud! Turn it down!

He grabs her and dances her round the room, singing loudly to himself. This upsets her.

Shaun! I'm trying to get to sleep up there! Turn it down will you?

Marti *enters in the doorway with* **Dean**. **Shaun** *sees him and stops. He stares at* **Marti**. **Clarine** *rubs her arms where he's gripped her a bit too tightly.* **Shaun** *grabs* **Marti** *to dance. He dances for a bit then stops, hugs* **Marti** *to him and cries.* **Marti** *leads him to the bed and lies him down.* **Shaun** *pulls him down on the bed and holds onto him, still crying.* **Dean** *and* **Clarine** *both watch this, then* **Dean** *leads* **Clarine** *out, shutting the door behind them as the music fades.*

Scene Four

A few days later. **Shaun** *is packing away all his possessions into an assortment of suitcases. He discards some items in the room and keeps others. There's no pattern to the packing. Sometimes he'll go in the kitchen and return with things from there.* **Marti** *sits on the couch with a pen and paper.* **Shaun** *is dictating a letter to him.*

Shaun   Dear Juliet,

How's Barbados? I hope your flight was turbulent and that all the air-hostesses were dykes and sexually harassed you. I hope the weather is really shite and that you get mugged at least seventeen point five times a day. I hope the funeral went disastrously and that there was some big cock-up and you ended up in the grave as well.

Marti   How d'you spell disastrously?

Shaun   Shut up. (*Continues.*) I just want you to know that I didn't enjoy a single second that I was with you. I ate kebabs behind your back. I was shagging George for six months. I faked every orgasm and since you've left have become a leading light in the British National Party.

Marti   Oh, that's sick.

Shaun   I said shut up. (*Continues.*) I was so delighted to hear that you'd finished with me that I threw a party and shagged loads of well tasty women. Linda Lusardi, the girl off the Peugeot adverts, Kate Moss and Björk.

Marti   Björk?

Shaun   Shut it. (*Continues.*) I forgot to mention that I am HIV positive.

Marti   Ay!! Now I'm not playing any more. (*Throws pad down.*)

Shaun   And as we never practised safe sex, you probably are as well by now.

Marti   Even if you faked every orgasm?

Shaun   I've never met anybody as ugly as you in my life, and if I ever do again I hope I don't take pity on them because I think it would have been better for both of us, and especially you, if I had taken a machete to your ugly face the day I met you. The grand you invested in Curls on Wheels I have spent on hiring a contract killer to slaughter all your family on Boxing Day . . . 1999. I hope you are ill. Lots of hate. Badbye. Shaun.

Marti And who says we people in Liverpool can't take a knock?

Shaun It's just a shame I don't know where she is.

Marti I think you're being stupid.

Shaun Marti, I can't send her that.

Marti No. This stupid idea of yours to move back to Liverpool. There's no room in me mam and dad's house. They'll drive you up the wall.

Shaun So far I have driven up that wall, across that ceiling and down the other side being here.

Marti But the business . . .

Shaun If it's the five hundred quid you're worried about then I'll pay you back.

Marti You can't afford that.

Shaun I can borrow it.

Marti Off who?

Shaun I'll send it to you.

Marti I'm not worried about the five hundred quid. I'm not a capitalist bastard, am I?

Shaun Aren't you? I dunno. You just seem a bit bothered about the bloody van.

Marti I don't give a shit about the van, Shaun.

Shaun Well, stop mithering me then.

Marti Moving back to Liverpool's a backward step. You wanna move forward. Onwards and upwards.

Shaun I'm not staying here.

Marti   Come and stay wit me.

Shaun   I just. I just need some time on me own to chill. Every street I walk down round here's got Juliet written all over it. I'm sick of heartache when I see . . . when I see the bench we sat on or the, or the bloody pizza place we went to. I'm doing meself in with it all. Anyway. I like Liverpool.

Marti   You left it soon enough.

Shaun   To go on some big adventure. To find me. Well, I didn't find me, I found her. Oh. It's not forever, is it. Might only be a few months. Or weeks. When London's knocking the shite and stuffing outa yer, where d'you go for a breather?

Marti   Brighton.

Shaun   You go back to your ma and da's, you know you do.

Marti   I'd hate to see you take such a big fall backwards coz of some snobby bitch.

Shaun   A week, a month, a year, it's neither here nor there. I'm doing it.

Marti   You can take the girl from Liverpool, but you can't take Liverpool from the girl.

Shaun   When you've split up with anyone in the past, what've you done eh? You moved on to a different city.

Marti   I didn't know you then.

Shaun   Well, it's true, isn't it?

Marti   I don't want to talk about it.

Shaun   Why not? I'll tell you why not, coz you know deep down I'm doing the right thing.

Marti   But you're stronger than me.

Shaun   Marti, we're from the same stock you and me. I'm not.

Marti   Go back to Liverpool. See if I care.

Shaun   You're . . . you're . . .

Marti   I said go back to Liverpool. With my consent.

Shaun   But, Marti, I don't need your consent. I'm not your boyfriend.

Marti (*American*)   Oh, really? I didn't know.

Shaun   Well, sometimes I feel that . . . oh, what's the point.

Shaun *goes into the kitchen.*

Marti   What have you felt?

Shaun (*off*)   Nothing.

Marti   That I'm in love wit yer?

Shaun (*off*)   Oh, forget I said anything, Marti. (*Returns with plates.*)

Marti   And what if I was?

Pause.

Shaun   Don't be daft.

Marti   I spent most of me life hating you. Why can't I spend the rest of it loving you?

Shaun   Shut up.

Marti   You were such a homophobic little bastard.

Shaun   No, I wasn't.

Marti   I know.

Shaun   Well, then.

Marti   I do. I know. That's my problem. D'yer ever feel you were blessed with the gift of insight? I do. And even as I lay there in the hospital, blood oozing from every orifice. I knew you didn't really mean it. It's only coz you were young. I knew it wasn't your fault, though it didn't help.

Shaun   I was a prick then and I've changed.

Marti   It didn't stop me hurting.

Shaun   Marti.

Marti   Shut up, will yer? I'm talking here. I never knew the real you.

Pause.

Shaun   No one did. I was the hardknock coz I felt . . . I felt. Oh, you know the other day, when you said you'd built up the camp bit to protect you from the knocks? Well, that's what I did with me fists.

Marti   And then Juliet's on the scene and suddenly you're Romeo. And I'm all right. Welcomed in with open arms. But I knew.

Shaun   God, you know everything you, don't yer?

Marti   I know you. I've known you since you were an egg. It was all her doing. You were nothing 'til you met her and now you're nothing again. And now I'm nothing.

Shaun   Don't say that, Marti.

Marti   All the time. I wanted yer all to meself. And now I've got it. And it's not what I want at all. I find it hard to love you. I find it so hard it fucks me up. The only men I've ever loved have been fellas, my fellas. I never loved me dad. I never loved you once you were older. I wasn't allowed.

Shaun   But yer are now.

Marti   Shaun, I can't love you.

Pause.

Shaun   Now who's being homophobic? Can't love me coz I'm your own brother and you're a queen?

Marti   I don't know any straight men.

Shaun   You know me.

Marti   You're our kid.

Pause.

Shaun   The good thing about Juliet. She blew me brains away wit knowledge and understanding and tolerance . . .

Marti   Oh, so I'm to be tolerated, am I?

Shaun   I'm not articulating this very . . . just . . . Credit me with some sense man. I'm not gonna drop everything we've got coz of her!

Pause.

What?

Marti   I'm not used to it.

Shaun   What?

Marti   Someone loving me.

Shaun *goes and sits on the arm of the sofa and cuddles* **Marti**. **Marti** *is crying.* **Shaun** *lifts his face up and wipes the tears off his face. He holds* **Marti**'s *hands.*

Marti   I do love yer, you know.

Shaun   Then stop fucking crying.

Marti *kisses him. It's half a snog. They have a snog for a split second.* **Marti** *pulls away.*

Marti   Jesus Christ, what've I done?

Shaun   It's all right, lad.

Shaun *stands.*

Shaun   I better get me stuff from the bathroom.

He exits through the main door. **Marti** *sits there gasping for breath. He looks around him panicking. He has difficulty sitting still. He gets up and goes to the window and batters it. He runs off to the kitchen and we hear a lot of banging about, drawers and doors. Then finally a quick smash of broken glass.*

Shaun *comes back in with a red towel.*

Shaun   It's pointless taking a half-empy bottle of Wash and Go back with me. Listen, lad, will you fly that kettle on while you're in there?

He lifts a suitcase onto the bed to close it. **Marti** *comes to the door of the kitchen holding his wrists, they're bleeding. He has slashed his wrists on the kitchen window. He stands there hysterically half laughing/half crying.* **Shaun** *hears and turns around. He is immobilised, staring at* **Marti**.

Marti   I don't. I don't.

Marti *looks about him not knowing what to do. He goes to the window and pulls the blind down. He turns to* **Shaun**. **Shaun** *gets up and gets a cigarette. He holds it in his hand, trembling. There is a tap on the main door and* **Clarine** *enters. She is dressed as in the first scene and carrying her guitar. She speaks with a London accent.*

Clarine   Hiya, darling.

Shaun *is staring at* **Marti**. *He lifts the cigarette to his mouth and lights it.* **Clarine** *looks around and sees* **Marti**. *She drops the London accent.*

Clarine   Oh, my God. (*To* **Shaun**.) Have you phoned for help?

She gets no response. She goes to the phone and dials 999.

(*On phone.*) Ambulance. (*Beat.*) Yeah. Ambulance please. Fifteen Rupert Street. Middle flat. There's been an incident. (*Beat.*) An incident. Quickly please.

She puts the phone down. She throws the guitar down on the sofa and goes out to the kitchen.

Marti (*to* **Shaun**)   Shut it, will yer? (*Beat.*) I said shut up.

Clarine *rushes back in with wet tea towels and ties them round* **Marti**'*s wrists.*

Clarine   You're gonna be all right, love. You're gonna be okay.

Marti   Yeah.

Clarine   Isn't he, Shaun? You're gonna be just fine. There, there's nothing to worry about. Come on.

She leads him to the couch and sits down with him.

That's it. Everything's gonna be fine. I'm here. Shaun's here. Everything's gonna be okay.

Marti *is looking at the guitar and nodding to it. He is crying in pain now.* **Shaun** *sits on the bed smoking in a daze.* **Clarine** *picks up the guitar.*

Clarine   Isn't it lovely?

Marti   Yeah.

Clarine   You like musical instruments, don't you?

Marti   Yeah.

Clarine   Ah, so do I! Listen. (*She strums a chord. He smiles. She strums again.*)

Marti   Yeah.

Clarine *strums an intro to 'House of the Rising Sun'.*

Marti   Yeah.

Clarine *starts to sing. As she does* **Marti** *sits back and leans his head back.* **Shaun** *continues to smoke.*

Clarine   Amazing Grace
How sweet the sound
That saved a wretch like me.
I once was lost
But now am found
Was blind and now can see.

The tea towels are now red with blood. The lights fade. As the blackout comes, 'Miss Chatelaine' by k. d. lang starts to play.

Boom Bang-A-Bang

Boom Bang-A-Bang was first performed at the Bush Theatre, London, on 19 July 1995, with the following cast:

Lee	Chris Hargreaves
Wendy	Jane Hazlegrove
Steph	Gary Love
Roy	Francis Lee
Tania	Elaine Lordan
Nick	Karl Draper
Norman	Rob Jarvis

Directed by Kathy Burke
Designed by Robin Don
Lighting by Paul Russell
Sound by Paul Bull
Costumes by Becky Hewitt

Characters

Lee, *about thirty, soft Liverpudlian accent.*
Wendy, *his younger sister, late twenties.*
Steph, *early thirties, camp male Londoner.*
Roy, *about twenty, from Rochdale.*
Tania, *late twenties, loud north Londoner.*
Nick, *her boyfriend, possibly a bit younger, slight Northern accent. An actor often typecast as a wife batterer.*
Norman, *about thirty, ugly Liverpudlian, lives upstairs from Lee.*

Setting

The play is set in the lounge of Lee's Kentish Town flat on the night of the 1995 Eurovision Song Contest.

There's a three-piece suite, a glass-topped coffee-table, a chest of drawers housing a modern stereo at the back of the room, an old television at the front of the room. On one wall a mirror, on another a blown-up photograph in a clipframe of a man who bears a striking resemblance to Johnny Logan. There's a radiator at the back as well which has hanging on it a mini clothes-horse with a few T-shirts drying on it. Another small table houses a few bottles of mineral water, brandy, wines and fruit juice. Two doors, one to the kitchen, one to the hall etc. Another door, glass, next to the window, which leads out on to the balcony. We must be able to see out of this. On the wall next to the hall door there is an entryphone and buzzer, which lets people into the flat. His proper phone sits on the floor next to one of the armchairs.

Act One

As the lights come up we see **Lee** *in casual clothes and slippers, placing some bowls of nuts on the coffee-table. The stereo is on and he is playing his Eurovision Song Contest medley tape. 'Boom Bang-A-Bang' by Lulu is playing. He inspects the room, then goes off to the kitchen. He returns with a few ashtrays and places them at strategic points around the room. There is a knock on the door. He looks suspiciously at the door then goes and opens it to* **Norman**, *the bloke who lives above him.* **Norman**'*s no oil painting, and speaks quite slowly in a Liverpool accent stronger than* **Lee**'*s. He is carrying an armchair a lot less stylish than* **Lee**'*s taste.*

Norman Any room at the inn, girl? Hiya.

Lee Oh hiya, Norman.

Norman Another chair and you're almost there!

Lee Oh thanks, Norman.

Lee *helps* **Norman** *carry the armchair in and they arrange it at an appropriate part of the room.*

Norman Well, another chair and you are there really. Hey, you've got it looking nice in here, haven't you eh? Eh?

Lee Thanks.

Norman It's a transformation. It's a make-over. It's a before and after. It is! I mean, between you me and the shag (*Indicates carpet.*) the people who were here before you. They didn't know the first thing about decor. I think to them, decor was a foreign word.

Lee Ah, thanks a lot for this, Norman. I really appreciate it.

Norman Well, you see, Lee. I know what it's like when you're doing the entertaining. If you've got nowhere to sit everyone you're fucked. Ah, I hope yous have a fabulous time anyway.

Lee Thanks. You going out tonight?

Norman   No. I think I'll just sit in and mong around the flat. Have something to eat and . . . (*Sniffs.*) . . . ooh, something smells nice.

Lee   Garlic bread. Listen, Norman –

Norman   Ooh, it's nice that, isn't it? Hey, you don't know how many minutes it takes to do a pot noodle, do yeh?

Lee   Won't it say on the side?

Norman   Spose. (*He's seen the photo on the wall.*) Ah, was that him?

Lee   Yes.

Norman   Mm. He doesn't half remind me of someone.

Lee   I mean, all the people coming tonight were quite close to him. I mean I'd love to invite you down, but –

Norman   Now who does he remind me of?

Lee   I mean it's a sort of tradition we've always had. Getting together to watch the Eurovision. I know it sounds silly.

Norman   I'm a great stickler for tradition meself. Is that a new telly?

Lee   No.

Norman   Mm. I've just bought a new one. Eighteen-inch screen, dolby sound system and a thingy –

Lee   Remote?

Norman   Control. Oh, it's marvellous you know. Set me back a bob or two, mind. Speakers everywhere.

Lee   This is ancient. Sentimental value really.

Norman   Oh God, tell me about it, you wanna see the state o'my stereo. But it was me Aunty Edie's, you know. Knocked her head on a downspout and never woke up. Death, it's dead . . . final. Isn't it?

Pause.

Oh well. Back upstairs. To me place on the shelf. Enjoy your meal. And your party.

Lee   It's not really a party.

Norman (*sees the clothes-horse*)   Oh God, look at that, isn't it gorgeous?

Lee   Oh, I've been meaning to put that away.

Norman   Oh, where'd you get this? (*Runs his hands over it.*)

Lee   Er, it was a present.

Norman   Goway! Oh, it's really nice, isn't it? You got a washing-machine?

Lee   Yeah.

Norman   Tumble-drier?

Lee   Yeah, but I'm just airing these.

Norman   Dunno where I'd be without mine.

Lee   The launderette probably.

Norman (*without laughing*)   D'you know what? That's funny that is. And d'you wanna know why? Coz it's the Liverpool sense of humour. And down here us Scousers should stick together coz I'll tell you this for nothing, Lee. There are some really boring people in London. And that's no word of a lie. B. O. R. I. N. G. Boring. I can't get over it, you know.

Lee   I should be getting on really.

Norman   Well, if there's anything you need just give us a shout.

Lee   Okay then.

Norman (*sniffs again*)   It's good for you garlic, you know.

Lee   I know.

Norman   Might put some in my pot noodle coz I think I'm coming down with something terrible.

Lee   See you.

Norman   Trar, kidder.

Norman *exits.* **Lee** *brushes some dust off* **Norman**'s *chair. His sister* **Wendy** *enters from the kitchen. She is smoking a joint.*

Lee   Norman. Upstairs.

Wendy   I've badly mistimed this garlic bread.

The door buzzer goes. **Lee** *gets up and goes to the wallphone.*

Wendy   It's nearly ready.

Lee   We can always bung it in the microwave later. (*To phone.*) Hello? Oh hi, Steph, push the door. We're on the first floor. (*Replaces the receiver.*) Steph.

Wendy (*not impressed*)   Steph.

Wendy *swiftly exits to the kitchen.* **Steph** *appears from the hall. He speaks fast and officiously, and is wearing an overcoat and carrying a bottle of wine and a bumbag. He has brought a huge picture in a frame wrapped in pink crêpe paper as a house-warming present. He plonks the bottle of wine down on* **Lee**'s *drinks table and looks around the room.*

Lee   My new abode.

Steph   I thought it'd be bigger than this.

Lee   Well –

Steph   Had a picture of it in my head.

Lee   Size isn't everything.

Steph   No, it's what you do with it. And if you don't mind me saying you seem to have done with it reasonably well. Oh, a balcony. How sixties. (*Looks out of window.*) That Hampstead Heath?

Lee   Yeah.

Steph   Handy. For those late-night walks.

Lee   I find all that a bit of a bore really.

Steph   When you're bored with the Heath m'darling, you're bored with life.

Lee   Oh, I'm not bored with that just yet.

Steph   Pleased to hear it. *Pour vous, s'il vous plaît.*

He hands **Lee** *the house-warming picture.*

Lee   Oh, Steph, there was no need . . .

Steph   Nonsense, it's house-warming, init?

Lee (*joking, shaking it*)   Is it a jigsaw?

Steph   No, it's a picture. Get it opened.

Lee *rests the picture on his settee and rips open the crêpe paper. It is a Tom of Finland print showing a man with a huge penis.* **Lee** *thinks it is vile but daren't say.* **Steph** *is beaming.*

Lee   Oh, Steph . . .

Steph   I thought of you as I seen it you know. I said to the man in Clone Zone, I said, 'You know this is *so* Lee.'

Lee   Oh, it's . . . yeah . . .

Steph   It's gorgeous, isn't it?

Lee   It's a bit big, isn't it?

Steph   Well, you've the length of wall fortunately. Look good over the telly actually. Do I get a kiss?

Lee   Cheers, Steph. (*Kisses him.*)

Steph (*suggestively*)   You gonna take my coat?

Lee   Where to? (*Laughs.*)

Steph (*taking coat off*)   It's nice to see you smile again, Lee. You suit it. Mourning didn't suit you. I hate to see a man frown. (*Passing coat to* **Lee***, he grasps hold of* **Lee***'s hand and speaks in a faster, hushed conspiratorial tone.*) Top Man in Oxford Street. Get your arse down there. Communal changing rooms. I was in for hours. Had to buy this to keep the store detectives happy. Not a big fan of store detectives. Are you?

Lee   Can't say I am.

Steph   No, me neither. (*The wine.*) New Zealand. Thought you might like a drop of Maori in you.

Lee   Oh tar. I'll just . . . stick this in the bedroom. Might get in the way a bit.

Steph *winks.* **Lee** *exits to the hall with* **Steph**'s *coat and the picture.* **Steph** *sits and gets cigarettes out of his bumbag. He has to root around to find them, and in so doing gets out a pair of handcuffs and some nipple clamps, which he returns to the bumbag as he lights up.*

Steph   Is this your Eurovision medley tape?

Lee (*off*)   Yes.

Steph   Thought so. (*Looking around room.*) Actually you know, this is spesh. *Bijou,* but *très* spesh.

Lee (*off*)   I can run you a copy off if you want.

Steph   That's kind of you. (*Pause. He's having a good nose around.*) How's that vile bitch from hell Wendy? Is she out of that wheelchair yet?

Wendy (*off*)   Yes, I am, thanks for asking!

Wendy *enters from the kitchen, lurking in the doorway with a roll-up.*

Steph (*thinking very quickly*)   Just my joke! Knew you were here. Hi, Wend. Smelt your perfume.

Wendy   Hello, Steph.

Steph (*kissing her*)   Terrible accident, Wend. So I heard. Lee showed me the clipping from the *Bromley Gazette.* You could've died, couldn't you, Wend?

Wendy   Well . . .

Steph   All that crazy paving stacked up one minute. Next thing you're under it. Suppose it was like dominoes, wasn't it? One goes, they all go. Not nice.

Wendy   No.

Steph   No. And my heart bleeds for you, Wendy. Every time you look out your window you gotta look at that damn patio. Did you manage to scrape all the blood off the crazy paving?

Wendy   Yeah. I get the pins taken out on Thursday.

Steph   Great. Great. No, that is great actually, Wend. You're up and about at last and that's great. Wasn't aware that you were a fan of the Eurovision actually.

Lee *enters.*

Lee   Wendy didn't have anything to do, so . . .

Steph   I thought of you the other day actually. I saw a woman in a wheelchair in Marks and I thought 'I wonder how Wendy is?'

Wendy   That was kind of you. I'm just going to check the garlic bread.

Wendy *exits.*

Steph (*quieter, more urgently so* **Wendy** *doesn't hear*)   You might have told me.

Lee   I was about to.

Steph   I wanna get on with your family, even if they are vile.

Lee   Oh, thanks.

Steph   Well, how you and her could have sprung from the same womb I'll never know.

Lee (*tuts*)   Steph.

A look of horror covers **Steph**'s *face.*

Steph   Oh, Lee, I'm sorry. I forgot you were one of Barnardo's finest.

Lee   Forget it, it's okay.

Steph   All the same I don't see the point in having a Eurovision Song Contest party and inviting people who don't know their Clodagh Rogers from their Jahn Teigen. It's ridiculous.

Lee   She'll enter into the spirit of things, don't you worry.

Steph   This night is the highlight of my year if you must know. (*Jovially.*) You'll be telling me you've invited Nick and Tania next. (*Pause. He gets more serious.*) You haven't.

Lee   Well, loads of people dropped out.

Steph   Nick and . . . ? I don't believe it!

Lee   Oh, they're lovely.

Steph   Oh, really!

Lee   Nick has been a tower of strength to me lately.

Steph   I bet he has.

Lee   Steph!

Steph   Well, it's a bit rich if you ask me.

Lee   Well, I didn't.

Pause.

Steph   I'da come round at the drop of a hat if I wasn't working.

Lee   I know.

Steph   I read this article the other day in this magazine. 'Straight Men Who Suck Dick.' It sounded like a character description of Nick.

Lee   God, Steph, I don't understand you at times.

Steph   Yeah, well, what's new? Pour me a wine.

Lee   Red or white?

Steph   Surprise me.

Lee *goes about trying, with some difficulty, to open the wine* **Steph** *brought.*

Steph   Has he ever watched a Eurovision Song Contest?

Lee   Probably.

Steph   But you don't know for sure.

Lee   No.

Steph   The key to a perfect Euro evening, Lee, m'darling, is relaxation. I can't stress that strongly enough. And if there are non Eurovision fans present we'll feel oppressed.

Lee   I won't.

Steph   I will. They'll talk through the songs.

Lee   Well, that's part of the fun.

Steph   Part of the fun, Lee, my darling, is being amongst friends. Fellow enthusiasts. (**Wendy** *has come in with her joint which has gone out.*) Did you know Nick was coming?

Wendy   Yes. Got a light? This has gone out.

Steph (*passing his lighter*)   I'm just . . . I'm just a bit on edge if you must know. Ignore me.

Wendy   Something wrong?

Steph   You wouldn't understand.

Wendy   Try me.

Steph   For the first time in Eurovision history we have a rap group representing us. Okay, so it's a novelty. Last time we won we did so on the novelty of the Bucks Fizz skirt rip. But what I'm beginning to get a tad anxious about is . . . what if nobody likes it? What if we get *nul points*? We won't be able to take part in next year's contest if we come in the final four. And that would be a catastrophe . . . See? I told you you wouldn't understand.

Lee (*having no success with opening the wine. Offers it to* **Wendy**) Can you have a go at this? (**Wendy** *tries to open the bottle.* **Lee** *looks at his watch.*) Twenty past seven. Excited?

Steph   I suppose so. So who else is coming?

Lee   Er, well . . .

Wendy   Nick and Tania.

Lee   Roy . . .

Steph   Roy? Very good. At least if we lose we've got something nice to look at.

Lee   And that's it I think.

Pause. **Steph** *looks confused.*

Steph   But what about all the others?

Lee   Well, Billy's having people round to his.

Steph   Billy's not coming here?

Wendy (*shakes head*)   Throwing his own do.

Steph   Well, what about Alan and Kevin? They'll be coming here surely.

Lee   Going to Billy's apparently.

Steph   But. I don't under . . . last year there were twenty or thirty of us.

Wendy   Steph.

Steph   What?

Lee   It's all right, Wend.

Steph   What?

Lee   I think people would rather go to Billy's this year.

Steph   Well, I think I would too from the sound of things.

Lee   I don't think people wanna come her coz of Michael.

Pause.

Steph   Well, it didn't stop me.

Lee   I know. And I'm glad. I mean that, Steph. I'm glad you've come here. We could've all gone to Billy's but, I just wanted to be in me own place.

Wendy   Far from the madding crowd.

Lee   Maybe next year I'll fancy going somewhere else.

Wendy (*giving up on bottle*)   The cork's buggered. You'll have to use a knife.

Lee *goes into the kitchen.*

Steph   I saw Billy in Sainsbury's last night. I thought his trolley looked a bit full. Thought he'd started seeing somebody. Should've known. Didn't breathe a word of it to me. Ignorant bastard, I've never liked him.

Wendy   Well, obviously the feeling's mutual.

Steph   Well, if he's not gonna come here just coz Michael's popped his clogs I don't think I want him liking me. Bellringers, never trust 'em.

Wendy   I think some people just don't know what to say.

Steph   Well, they should make something up. Poor Michael.

Wendy   Poor Lee.

Steph   Had a terrible row with Michael last year. I said Frances Rufelle was far superior to that Irish pair that won. He was having none of it.

Wendy   Didn't see you at the funeral.

Steph   I was in Tenerife. I was all set to cancel but Lee insisted I go.

Wendy   Not much of a tan to show for it.

Steph   I was in bed a lot.

Wendy   Diarrhoea?

Steph   Dream on, Wendy.

Lee *enters with three glasses of wine. He hands them out.*

Lee   We have a result. *Douze points*! Cheers.

Wendy   Cheers.

Steph   Cheers, Lee. I hope Nick and Tania aren't going to be late. There's nothing worse than having the first song obliterated by straight people taking their coats off. No offence, Wend.

Wendy   I'll check my bread.

She exits.

Lee   She can't help being straight.

Steph   If you ask me she's borderline Lebanese.

Lee   What's got into you?

Steph   She's the first straight woman I've met that can play pool.

Lee   Oh, fucking hell, Steph. How d'you explain that fella she was seeing?

Steph   Smokescreen. I could spot it a mile off.

Lee (*laughs*)   You're good value, I'll give you that!

Steph   Well, if she starts wearing sandals and humming Patsy Cline don't say I didn't warn you. So, it's still all on with Nick and Tania, is it?

Lee   Yeah.

Steph   Well, I wish they'd make their minds up and save us all the heartache.

Lee   They have made their minds up.

Steph   Yeah, but how long's it gonna last this time? I wouldn't be surprised if they've split up by the time Croatia are on.

Lee   They'll be fine. We'll all be fine.

Steph   Yeah, well, I think you're forgetting Abergavenny. It was like sharing a caravan with Barry McGuigan and . . . some other bloody boxer. Fight fight fight, and they call that love. Yeah, well, if that's love, you can take it, put it in a bin-bag and drop it in a very huge skip.

Lee   You don't mean that.

Steph   If I want personal fulfilment I just hang around the Coleherne at closing time. You can get whatever you want at those traffic lights, it's better than IKEA.

Lee   I couldn't.

Steph   Bollocks, you like hot sex like the rest of us m'darling. Hot sex is a prerequisite to happiness. I'm very safe, don't get me wrong, but there's never a dull moment in my life believe you me.

Lee   And where does love fit into the picture?

Steph   I'm not knocking love, I'm just saying that till you find it you should get some hot sex. It's the nature of the beast m'darling. The human machine has three carnal drives: to eat, to shit, and to mate: I love restaurants, I love a good crap and I like hot sex. I'm completely normal.

Lee   At least you're honest about it.

Steph   You'll find no skeletons in my closet. Scuse language. Mind you, I'm getting on a bit now. I quite fancy a shot at monogamy.

Lee   D'you think you're capable of it?

Steph   Course I bloody am. (*Winces.*) My right nipple.

Lee   What?

Steph   Red raw.

Pause.

Chewed to buggery last night. Nice bit of trade from the footwear industry. I sat him down, his name was Dave. Was it Dave? No, it was Darren. I sat him down and I said, 'Darren, I'm into non-penetrative safe sex.' It's so refreshing to have trade who understand four syllable words.

Lee   I couldn't imagine going to bed with anyone just yet. Me head's chocka.

Steph   Oh, they'll come crawling out of the woodwork for you. You must have a nice little nest egg if you don't mind me saying.

Lee   Michael left me a bit.

Steph   I know the sort of money architects earn. All I'm saying is be careful. There's some who'll be after you for it . . . whereas if it was me . . .

Lee   You'd be after me for me devastating looks and personality?

Steph   Why not?

Lee   I know you too well.

Steph   Oh, everyone thinks they know me. When really. No one knows no one. Anybody. Whatever.

Pause.

His name wasn't Darren last night it was Delyth. Welsh piece.
(*Beat.*) How's Norman No-Mates upstairs?

Lee   Fine.

Steph   Still pestering you?

Lee   A bit.

Steph   Well, be grateful you've got a queen on top of you. I've
got heterosexuals either side and if it's not R.E.M. it's Lou
Bloody Reed morning noon and night.

Lee   That's his chair.

Steph   And what does *he* look like?

Lee   A cross between Marty Feldman and Mr Bean.

Steph   I might have to pop up there later. The ugly ones are
often so much better in bed. More desperate. More . . .

The door buzzer goes.

Lee   That's probably Roy. (**Lee** *goes to wallphone.*) Hello? Come
on up Roy. The door's on the latch.

Wendy (*off*)   Is that Roy?! (*Enters.*)

Steph   Gonna make him straight, are you, Wend? Gonna show
him the pins in your knee?

The door opens. **Roy** *enters. He's a lot younger than everyone else and has a
Rochdale accent. He wears a ravey get-up, tight T-shirt with his belly-
button showing, jeans and a coat that looks like a sheepskin rug, he carries a
bunch of flowers and a bag of booze, he enters the room and starts dancing,
singing 'Love City Groove' by Love City Groove.*

Roy (*sings*)   In the morning, when the sun shines.
Down on your body,
And now we're really making love now baby.

(*Speaks.*) We're not gonna win, are we? We're gonna be a
laughing stock, aren't we? I'm convinced. Hiya.

Steph   Hi, Roy.

Wendy   Roy.

Roy Give us a hug you. (*Hugs* **Lee**.) I bought you these. (*Gives him the flowers*.)

Lee Ah, they're lovely. What a sweetie. Oh, aren't they nice?

Steph Got anything for me, Roy? Like a peck on the cheek?

Roy I've got a coleslaw. How's your leg, Wendy?

Wendy Fine. They're coming out on Thursday.

Roy Marvellous. (*He gets champagne and orange juice out of his bag*.) Champagne and orange juice, thought we could all have a Bucks Fizz.

Wendy Oh, brilliant. Let me . . . (*She takes them off him. To* **Lee**.) Shall I put those in water? (*She takes the flowers*.)

Lee Tar, Wend.

Wendy Right, I'll rustle something up in the kitchen.

Steph She knows her place.

Wendy (*exiting*) Put a personality on the top of your next shopping list, Steph.

Roy *laughs uproariously*. **Wendy** *has gone into the kitchen*.

Roy How are you feeling, Steph?

Steph Well, hardly 'Rock Bottom' now you've arrived.

Lee Sit down.

Roy I can't I'm too excited. (*Starts to dance on the spot*.) I was gonna take an E before I came but I thought no, I'm gonno enjoy this straight. I'm thinking of going to Trade after this, anyone coming?

Steph Now there's a thought.

Roy Lee?

Lee I don't think so.

Roy Ah, will you be too depressed if we don't win?

Lee It's not that. I'm off clubs at the moment.

Roy Well, fair enough.

Steph   I might be up for that Roy.

Roy   Bona. Bonerata! What time is it?

Lee   Twenty-five past.

Roy   Whoo!! Not long now. Ay, int your sister lovely?

Lee   Yeah.

Roy   Int she lovely, Steph?

Steph   Unique.

Roy   I know. I was down the Black Cap the other week and Lee dragged her along and we gabbed all night. Oh, I think she's fab.

Steph   You've started going to the Black Cap?

Lee   Yeah.

Steph   Didn't realise that was your scene.

Roy   It's been refurbished.

Steph   Oh, you must let me know the next time you go, I worship the Black Cap.

Roy   Eh, we'll all go one night and have a laugh.

Steph   Yeah, that would be phenomenal actually.

Roy   Ah, yeah!

Steph (*to* **Lee**)   You're off clubbing but you'll go to the Black Cap. Forgive me for appearing ignorant, but isn't there a little inconsistency in your rationale there?

Lee   We just went for a few drinks.

Steph   I seem to recall leaving a few messages on your answerphone drinkswise but you never got back.

Lee   This was a spur of the moment thing.

Steph   Oh, well, you know who your friends are.

Lee   Since Michael died I've preferred an early night, that's all. This particular night I didn't.

Steph   Roy, will you sit down please? You're making me nauseous.

Roy   Don't you think I'm a good dancer? I won a tennis racquet once in the youth club disco dance championships.

Steph   A tennis racquet, Roy? That's handy.

Roy   Me bastard brother broke it the next day. Smashed it over his girlfriend's head. She had to go to hospital and everything.

Steph   Heterosexual men. Never trust 'em.

Lee   Was she all right?

Roy   Yeah you could hardly notice the stitching on the wedding photos.

Wendy *enters with a tray. A jug and glasses of Bucks Fizz stand on the tray.*

Wendy   Bucks Fizz anybody?

Roy   Ah fab! Eh, Steph. Are you in two minds about this or are you 'Making your Mind Up'?! (*Laughs.*)

They all help themselves to a glass of Bucks Fizz.

Steph   'One Step Further' and I might be pissed!

Roy   I'd 'Beg Steal or Borrow' for a drink right now!

Lee (*raising glass*)   'Better the Devil You Know Than the Devil You Don't.'

Steph   Just quoting UK Eurovision song titles, Wendy. Hope you don't feel left out.

Wendy   I don't, Steph. And please don't 'Save Your Kisses for Me' tonight.

Pause.

Steph   I hear you've sampled the delights of the Black Cap, Wendy. Did all the queens shout 'Fish!' when you went in?

Wendy   No, and I didn't shout 'Cheese' at them.

Roy (*to* **Wendy**)   Ah, haven't you got a fab sense of humour? Ah, and you're dead pretty you know, dunno why you haven't got a boyfriend.

Steph   Coz she's a dyke.

Roy   Ah, leave her alone.

Wendy   What if I was?

Steph   Well, you're butch enough.

Roy   Copped off lately, Steph?

Lee   Last night.

Steph (*to* **Lee**)   Bless you, my darling.

Roy   Ah was he gorgeous? What was he like? How old was he?

Steph   Twenty-five? Circa twenty-five anyway.

Wendy   Name?

Steph   Danny.

Roy   Nice?

Steph   Mm, brought up in Bristol actually.

Wendy   Will you see him again?

Steph   No.

Roy   Would you like to?

Steph   No. And I didn't take a polaroid of him either before you ask.

Wendy   You wanna be careful, Steph.

Steph   I'm into non-penetrative safe sex, Wendy, actually.

Wendy   Well, I'd hate to open the paper one morning and see you've been butchered by an axe-wielding maniac.

Roy   I know.

Steph   Bless you, Wendy, what a special thought.

Wendy   You should always let someone know where you're going.

Steph   Would you like to give me a guided tour of your new flatette, Lee, my lovely?

Lee   Gladly.

Steph   Come on, fresh. (*Stands, to* **Wendy**.) Lee's just gonna give me a guided tour of his flat, Wendy. So if I don't come back either Lee's killed me or he's at least a witness. Okay?

Wendy   I'll look forward to it.

Steph   And hands off my bubbly.

Lee   This is the kitchen.

Lee *and* **Steph** *exit to kitchen.*

Roy   Ah, Wend, don't you look gorgeous tonight?

Wendy   I haven't made any extra special effort.

Roy   Ah, you look really special.

Wendy   Well, this lipstick's new.

Roy   I always wanted a big sister. Someone you could watch getting ready to go out. Painting their nails for 'em, plugging in their Carmen rollers. We used to watch *Tenko*, d'you remember *Tenko*? All them fabulous women.

Wendy   In the concentration camp?

Roy   Yeah, and me mam used to say, 'If you could choose one of the women from *Tenko* to be your big sister, who'd you choose?'

Wendy   Which one did you pick?

Roy   The Australian one.

Wendy   I remember. Vaguely.

Roy   Big piece, blond hair. You never see her now, do you?

Wendy   No.

Roy   No. Shame really coz she was dead nice. I think the Japs got her.

Lee *and* **Steph** *enter from the kitchen and go towards the hall door.*

Steph   Well, I've always been a big fan of pine. Okay, Roy?

Roy   Yeah.

Steph   Great guns.

Steph *and* **Lee** *exit to hall.*

Roy   He was in Tenerife when Michael died, want he?

Wendy   Yes.

Roy   It's not right that.

Wendy   I didn't miss him.

Roy   Who else is coming?

Wendy   Nick and Tania.

Roy   Ah, fab, I've not met them, have I?

Wendy   Well, they were at the funeral.

Roy   I spent all day with Michael's sister. I think she fancied me. Kept asking did I do sports.

Wendy   Funny place to pull, a funeral.

Roy   Still . . . Nick and Tania eh? I can't wait to meet that Nick. He looks gorgeous in that Tango advert. I've never met a real actor before. Oh, tell a lie. I met Gail Tilsley once when I were home coz she opened a new MFI round the corner to me mam's. She's good that Gail Tilsley, isn't she?

Wendy   Yes.

Roy   She's got a lovely head of hair on her. I think if I were going to do it with a woman it'd have to be her.

Lee *enters.*

Lee   Steph's abluting.

Roy   Ah, you all right, Lee?

Lee   Yeah, I'm fine.

Roy   Ah, great. What time are Nick and Tania getting here?

Lee   Soon.

Roy   Ah, fab. We're gonno have a great time, aren't we?

Lee   I hope so.

Roy   Ah, we will though. I love the Eurovision me. Well, that's how we got to be mates, int it? Coz I walked in the pub that night and saw you with your Michael and I thought he was Johnny Logan. Ah, he was the two ends of Johnny Logan, wasn't he?

Lee   He did look like him.

Roy   Ah, they coulda swapped heads, couldn't they, Wend?

Wendy   Yeah.

Roy   And I made an absolute pratteth of meself, dint I?

Lee   No!

Roy   Oh, I did though. Asking for his autograph.

Lee   It was funny.

Roy   On a beermat. God, I shoulda known when I heard him speak, he weren't Irish.

Lee   No.

Roy   Johnny Logan. Still, we couldn't stop gabbing could we?

Lee   No.

Roy   Gabbed all night.

Lee   Yeah.

Roy   He were special your Michael. He was.

Lee   He was to me.

Roy   Ah, he was lovely. He looks dead handsome on that photo.

Lee (*looks at photo on wall*)   Like a model.

Roy   Though that was before he lost that weight. I mean, he missed his opportunity there. Modelling and that. I mean, you never know, do you? I mean, look at Kate Moss. She had to start somewhere, and now she's practically running the country.

Wendy (*to* **Lee**)   Are you okay?

Lee   Yeah.

Pause.

Roy   Have I put me foot in it?

Lee   Not at all.

Roy   Tell me if I have.

Lee   You haven't.

Roy   It's a lovely picture. I used to be jealous.

Lee   Did you?

Roy   Yeah.

Lee   That's nice.

Roy   Yeah.

Steph *enters from toilet.*

Steph   I'm still alive, Wendy. You can stop worrying now.

He sits down and lights up a cigarette.

They don't make brown toilet paper, do they.

Nobody seems very interested.

Think about it. You wouldn't know when to stop.

Wendy   Oh, Steph, do you have to?

Wendy *hurries out to kitchen.*

Steph   Is it premenstrual?

Wendy (*off*)   No, it's bloody well not!!

Steph   Have you seen the time? Come on, Nick and Tania.

Lee   They'll get here.

Steph   Probably having a row in the middle of Camden High Street, as per.

Lee   No.

Steph   You drinking my wine, Lee?

Lee   What? Er, no, this is some that was left over from the other night.

Steph Lee?

Lee Mm?

Steph Tell Aunty Steph all the gory details please. Who were you drinking wine with?

Lee Nick.

Roy Nick and Tania?

Lee No, just Nick. I went to see him in a playreading in Richmond, then we came back here for wine and Pringles.

Steph And where was Tania? Had they had another row?

Lee No. She was visiting her mother.

Steph She didn't go to see his playreading?

Lee It was on for three nights, she went on the last night.

Steph So it was just you and Nick here on your own?

Lee Yes, Miss Marple.

Steph And . . . was the wine racy?

Lee Oh, shut up, Steph.

Steph Well, I do think it's a very odd friendship you have with that boy. You live in each other's pockets. Nick this, Nick that, Nick Nick Nick Nick Nick, I'm sick of the sound of him.

Lee What's odd about our friendship?

Steph Nothing, he's obviously an S.B.S.C.

Roy S.B.S.C.?

Steph Straight but sucks cock.

Lee There's nothing odd about a gay man and a straight man being mates.

Steph I think it's unnatural.

Roy I think it sounds dead nice.

Steph And nothing's happened between you two?

Lee Steph.

Steph   Well, I think there's something you're not telling us. It'll all end in tears.

Roy   D'you think all the groups'll be getting nervous now?

Lee   I really don't know, Roy.

Lee *exits to the kitchen.*

Steph   Methinks I hit a raw nerve.

Roy   If Nick was gay, why would he have a girlfriend?

Steph   Well, I slept with a woman once.

Roy   What was it like?

Steph   Nothing to write home about.

Roy   I wouldn't know what to do.

Steph   Close your eyes and think of Jason Orange.

Roy   I often wonder whether I've cut meself off. Whether I've put all me eggs in the one basket. Maybe I'm missing something.

Steph   Do something about it then.

Roy   There was this girl at Michael's funeral. It was his sister, Louise. She were dead pretty.

Steph   So?

Roy   We went round the back of the church hall and had a snog.

Steph   Did you like it?

Roy   It was all right.

Steph   Did you do anything else?

Roy   Two Es.

Steph   You really paid your respects, didn't you?

Roy   At least I was there.

Steph   You don't know how much I regret that. I love Lee. I hated every second of his mourning.

Roy   So why did you go to Tenerife then?

Steph   He insisted.

The door buzzer goes.

Roy   Have you seen Nick in that advert?

Steph   It's on often enough.

Lee *enters and goes to the wallphone.*

Roy   Don't you think he's gorgeous?

Lee (*to phone*)   Hello? Okay, push the door.

Steph   He's okay in a rough tradey sort of way.

Roy   Is it Nick and Tania?

Lee   Yeah.

Roy   Ah, fab.

Steph (*to* **Roy**, *about* **Lee**)   Look at him, he's all a quiver.

Lee   Shut up, Steph.

Steph   You are, you're trembling!

Lee   Will you just give it a rest, Steph? Please. Just. Give it a rest.

Steph   Okay okay.

Lee   Thank you.

Steph   Your secret's safe with me, Tania!!

Tania *enters with a petrol can with the lid missing.*

Tania   Oright? I couldn't bring Nick so I brung this. (*Laughs, holding the can up.*) He's parking the car. Has it started yet?

Lee   No, it doesn't start till eight.

Tania   I told him. He reckoned it was seven, stupid wanker. Oright, Steph?

Steph   Yeah, great guns.

Lee   This is Roy.

Tania   Oright?

Roy   Hiya.

Lee   This is Tania.

Roy   Hiya, Tania.

Tania (*gives* **Lee** *wine*)   And can you stick this somewhere, I don't want it stinking out my motor. (*Hands him can of pretrol as well.*) He's had it in there since he broke down the other night. You know he broke down, duntcha?

Lee   When?

Tania   When he came round here. Breakdowns, nothing new with him. Shouldna been driving anyway, state he was in. Can you stick it somewhere?

Lee *is putting the petrol can out on the balcony.*

Lee   Yeah, how's your mum? (*He spills some petrol on the balcony.*)

Tania   I don't wanna talk about it. Sorry, there's no lid on it.

Lee   I love the smell of petrol. (*Shutting balcony door.*) D'you wanna Buck's Fizz?

Tania   No, get us a lager.

Lee   Okay. (*Smells hands as he gets her a can of lager and starts pouring it into a glass.*)

Steph   I hear Nick's had some work.

Tania   Nick? Yeah, he done an episode o' *The Bill*.

Steph   Oh? I heard he'd been in a playreading.

Tania   Oh yeah, above a pub.

Steph   Any good?

Tania   No, it was crap. It was all about this fella called Jung, yeah? I felt totally ignorant watching it. He introduced me to the writer in the pub afterwards. I said, 'Listen, mate, don't give up the day job.'

Roy   Do you work?

Tania   Yeah. Cor, this is a nice suite, init? Where'd you get this?

Lee (*passing her a can and glass*)   Habitat.

Tania   Don't like that chair. (*She means* **Norman**'s.) Cheers, Lee, so we all watching this song contest shit, are we? Christ.

Steph   No one made you come.

Tania   Didn't they?

Roy   Aren't your shoes fab?

Tania   Yeah.

Wendy *enters.*

Wendy   Hiya, Tania, you all right.

Tania   Right, Wend? Eh, big day Thursday.

Roy   Oh, yeah, she's having her pins out.

Tania   I bet you can't wait, it's been months anit?

Wendy   Yeah, six.

Tania   National Health Service, they want shooting.

Wendy   Where's Nick?

Roy   Parking the car.

Tania   He'll be fucking hours. Good.

Steph   You two not getting on, Tania?

Tania   He's all right. In small doses.

Steph   Like thrush.

Tania   Yeah, 'cept if I chuck a tub o'live yoghurt on him he don't go away. (*Offers cigarettes.*) Anyone?

Roy *takes one, and* **Wendy** *takes another and sits to build a spliff.*

Roy   Tar.

Wendy   How's work?

Tania   Ah, God.

Roy (*to* **Lee**)   Where's she work?

Lee   Hospital.

Wendy   Tania's a psychiatric nurse.

Steph   Auxiliary, if you please.

Tania   We got this new bird started Tuesday. She fucking stinks. I went in that ward and I nearly keeled over with the smell. It was disgusting. I had to sort her out. I said, 'Listen love, I dunno whether you've heard of deodorant but you wanna fucking start using it.'

Lee   There's nothing worse, is there?

Wendy   And has she?

Tania   Says she don't believe in it, see. Says she wants to be how nature intended. I said 'Oh yeah? What's that? A smelly cunt?' I'll fucking deck her on Monday if she ant bucked her ideas up.

Roy   Is she a nurse? Or a patient?

Tania   Director of Finance. It's not on is it, Lee?

Lee   No, it's not.

The door buzzer goes.

Tania   Ignor it.

Lee *presses the button by the phone.*

Tania   Ask him about his audition today. He made a right prat of himself.

Roy   I've seen him in the Tango ads.

Tania   We had a gorgeous holiday out of the money from that. Fuerteventura. What were them pictures like I shown you, Wend?

Wendy   Oh, it looked idyllic.

Tania   It is a class restort. (*To* **Roy**.) What's your name?

Roy   Roy.

Tania   Roy, you have never seen water like it in all your life.

Roy   Blue?

Tania   Clear as crystal.

Nick *enters.*

Tania That was quick, get back out again we're not ready for you yet.

Nick Good evening. (*Kisses* **Lee**.)

Everyone greets **Nick**.

Lee Now you know everyone except Roy.

Nick (*shaking his hand*) Hello, Roy.

Roy Ooh, big hands! Hiya.

Tania I was just telling Roy about Fuerteventura.

Nick What a location, man.

Wendy Bucks Fizz, Nick? Or d'you want a can?

Roy What of? Tango?

Nick Er, Bucks Fizz, please. May as well slip into the character of the avid Song Contest fan.

Tania Nick?

Nick Mm?

Tania It starts at eight.

Nick Right.

Tania He thought it started at seven.

Roy (*to* **Nick**) If I move up, you can sit down.

Nick Thanks, Roy. So! What's new in Kentish Town?

Nick *joins* **Lee** *and* **Roy** *on the couch,* **Steph** *is in one armchair,* **Tania** *the other.* **Wendy** *will have* **Norman***'s chair. She pours* **Nick** *a glass of Bucks Fizz.*

Steph Hear you were in a fiasco of a playreading the other night, Nick. Tania says it was deplorable.

Nick Oh now, Tania, it wasn't that bad.

Roy What were it called? I might've heard of it.

Nick 'Psychodrama' by Chuck Finnegan. (*To* **Tania**.) You met him, didn't you, Babes?

Tania Chuck Finnegan? More like Chuck Up.

Nick It was quite meaty. The thing with playreadings is that you actually don't get much rehearsal time – a day if you're lucky – and then you're sort of semi-performing it.

Tania Nick, nobody's interested.

Roy I am.

Pause.

Roy I were in 'Dracula Spectacular' at senior school. I played Helga the tavern wench.

Pause.

Steph And you've done *The Bill* again?

Nick Yes.

Lee Fourth time.

Tania Tell them what you were playing.

Nick Barry Miles.

Tania Wife batterer.

Steph Again?

Tania Typecast, mate.

Nick No, this wife batterer was different. He'd been abused as a child.

Lee I don't remember that bit.

Nick Oh, it wasn't in the script. It was sort of unspoken. I got the penultimate line. 'There's no justice in this world.' And sort of sneered angrily at camera while that really great Asian WPC put the handcuffs on. She's delightful.

Wendy Is she? Yes, she looks nice.

Nick Well, they're all pretty cool. Great team. Great spirit. And bloody good.

Steph   Fascinating.

Lee   And you had an audition today?

Wendy   Oh, really? For what?

Nick   Danish sandwich spread.

Tania   Tell 'em what you had to be.

Nick   A wholemeal loaf. Medium sliced.

Tania   Ah, what a cunt! Who'd be an actor? Not me.

Lee   D'you think you'll get it?

Nick   Well, the director said he really liked my characterisation, so . . . fingers crossed.

Tania   Put the telly on, I'm bored.

Lee   It's not time yet.

Steph   I hope you're not gonna talk all the way through, Tania.

Tania   Nah, I'm looking forward to this. I love nothing better than sitting in a chair for three hours listening to crap music with words I don't understand and seeing the British fail miserably at everthing they do. Wend, you coming the pub?

Steph   That's not a bad idea actually.

Tania   You can't get rid of me that easily.

Nick   That's true.

Tania (*to* **Nick**)   Oi! Three thirty this morning, mate, you weren't complaining then. (*Winks at* **Roy**.)

Wendy   Roy's a big fan of yours, Nick.

Roy   Have you ever met Gail Tilsley? I have.

Nick   No. I did audition for the *Street* though, years back.

Roy   Really?

Lee   Yeah, to play thingy.

Nick   Medical student.

Lee   They said he was too old.

Tania   Well, they got tact, ant they.

Nick   You'll have to excuse Tania, her mother's not very well at the moment.

Pause.

Roy   Ah, what's wrong with her?

Wendy   Emphysema.

Nick   Tania's been under a lot of strain.

Tania   Shut up, Nick, nobody's interested.

Roy   I am.

Pause.

Roy   Is it fatal?

Pause.

Lee   I've made scoring cards.

Lee *goes to the chest of drawers and gets out some pieces of paper and some biros and starts giving them out.*

Lee   And we'll all need a pen.

Roy   D'you like the Eurovision, Nick?

Nick   My hobby's, like, experience. I think the only way you progress as a human being is by opening yourself up to new experiences.

Steph   Really?

Roy   It's been going forty years!

Nick   I'm really looking forward to this.

Roy   You're a lot taller. In the flesh.

Nick   You'll have to adjust your horizontal control.

Steph   Yeah, fiddle with your nob, sweetheart.

Tania   I'm starving. Any grub going?

Wendy   Five minutes.

Roy I always fancied being an actor. Did you have to go to drama college and learn how to do accents?

Nick You don't have to. There's plenty of guys around who are untrained and some of them, not all of them mind, are shit hot.

Lee You did though, didn't you.

Roy Do us a brummy accent, go on. I think it's dead difficult that one. I come out in Liverpool.

Nick (*Birmingham accent*) Y'oright, our kid? Hey, you looking forward to the Eurovision Song Contest, our kid?

Roy Ah, int that brilliant. It is, you know, it's brilliant that!

Tania Comes in handy, dunnit, Nick? For when you're down the pub with the luvvies and you can pretend you're a snobby git.

Wendy (*reading score card*) I didn't know Israel was in Europe.

Steph Course it bloody is. They won two years running.

Roy Seventy-eight and seventy-nine.

Lee 'A-ba-ni-bi' and 'Hallelujah'.

Steph Though between you and me I think their best entry was 'Halila', which is Israeli for 'Tonight'. It was performed by a group called Habibi, the lead singer of which was heavily pregnant.

Lee Eight months pregnant.

Steph Was it eight? I thought it was nine. Coz Terry Wogan said Habibi might be Havinababy. Yeah, I thought that was pretty droll actually.

Roy (*to* **Nick**) What drama college did you go to? Corona Kids?

Steph The RADA, wasn't it, Nick?

Nick RADA, yeah.

Steph The RADA, Roy. Pretty impressive, yep?

Roy I've heard of that. Isn't that where Julie Walters goes in *Prick Up Your Ears*?

Nick No, Gary Oldman. My hero.

Roy He got murdered, didn't he? By that one out of *Letter to Brezhnev*. And that one from *The Bill* finds them and then her out of *Howards End* buries the pair of them. I loved that movie, it were dead real.

Tania My pen don't work.

Lee Oh. (*Gets her another.*)

Nick I'm parked on a yellow line. I'll be all right, won't I?

Lee Yeah.

Steph You should've tubed it like me.

Lee Nick gets panic attacks on tubes.

Steph Since when?

Lee Since he got stuck on the Central Line for forty minutes in a tunnel. The lights went out and everything.

Steph Heaven.

Tania He's seeing an analyst.

Roy Ah, fab.

Lee He'll be all right, won't you, doll?

Nick Katriona's very pleased with my progress.

Roy Is she?

Steph Katriona?

Tania His analyst.

Roy Ah, fab.

Nick She's dutch.

Wendy Dutch?

Nick Yeah.

Steph You'll have to ask her if she knows Teach-In.

Lee Teach-In were a Eurovision group.

Steph A Dutch Eurovision group.

Roy   From Holland. They won as well.

Steph   Quite spectacularly actually, and with a fantastic song.

Lee   ⎫ Ding A Dong
Steph ⎬ Ding A Dong
Roy   ⎭ Ding Dang Dong

Steph (*to* **Roy**, *snapping*)   It was Ding A Dong!

Roy   It was Ding Dang Dong.

Steph   Lee?

Lee   It was Ding A Dong. I had the single.

Steph   B-side was 'Let Me In'.

(*Sings*.)   Let me in.
Don't say goodbye
Let me in
Oh me oh my.

Tania *yawns very loudly.*

Nick (*scolding*)   Tania?

Tania   Nicholas?

Wendy   Is the treatment counselling based?

Nick   For the time being. It's just such a relief to talk to someone who understands at last.

Tania   I understand.

Nick   A professional. My locum was useless.

Lee   Put him on Prozac.

Nick   Told me to grow up. I was disgusted.

Roy   Have you still got 'em?

Nick   The panic attacks?

Roy   No, the Prozac.

Nick   Chucked 'em.

Roy   Ah, I coulda sold them in the clubs.

Wendy (*reading scoring card*)   Lot of songs, aren't there?

Steph   There's only twenty-three.

Lee   It'll be over in the blink of an eye, Wend.

Tania   Good.

Nick   She's not really an analyst, she's an occupational therapist.

Steph   Well, let's face it, most actors go mad at some stage in their careers, Nick. Look at whatsisface . . .

Roy   Yeah.

Tania   Who?

Nick   I wouldn't say I was going mad exactly . . .

Steph   That one out of *Coronation Street*.

Roy   Gail Tilsley?

Steph   No.

Roy   I was gonna say! When I met her she didn't seem the slightest bit potty. She was ever so nice. She signed me a card. 'To Roy. Best Wishes, Helen Worth.' That's her name. She's very pretty in the flesh. I felt sorry for her. She was opening this new MFI and it was only me and me mam turned up to see her. They let her go early. Hey, just think, Nick, you coulda been in that and then I'd be sitting on the same couch as a *Street* star!

Tania   Shame he failed the audition really.

Lee   It's not really failure though, is it.

Roy   No.

Nick   No.

Wendy   More . . .

Steph   Losing.

Roy   Yeah.

Steph   Yeah.

Pause.

Nick (*to* **Tania**)   Babes? (**Tania** *looks over.*) Isn't that a cool picture of Michael?

Tania   Ah, Lee, you must be so happy you took that photo.

Lee   Wendy took it actually. Had her David Bailey hat on there.

Steph (*laughs uproariously*)   Hahaha! It's terrible!

Wendy⎫ Oh, shut up.
Nick ⎭ Have some fucking manners, Steph.

Tania   Yeah, Steph, be fair, that's a good picture.

Lee   It really captures something about him. I just look at it and . . . oh you know.

Tania   Yeah, Lee, I know exactly what you mean. To Michael. Miss you, you cunt. (*Raises glass.*)

All   To Michael!

Roy   Ah.

Tania (*going in her bag*)   Here, Lee, look what I found this morning. I was cleaning out the kitchen and this was down the back of the fridge. (*Gets postcard out of her bag.*) It's the postcard he sent me from Paris, right after he'd met you. (*Passes it round to him.*) Had a right little cry when I seen that.

Nick   Isn't that beautiful?

Lee   Yeah.

Tania   You can have that.

Nick   He was one happy man.

Tania   He was.

Nick (*puts his arm around* **Lee**)   You brought a lot of happiness into that guy's life. Don't be too hard on yourself.

Pause.

Nick   How was Tenerife, Steph?

Steph   Bloody hot if you must know.

Roy   Mandy Smith's been to Tenerife.

Tania   Has she?

Roy   Yeah.

Pause.

I'm reading her autobiography at the minute. No, she likes Spain. She likes the balmy heat and the mañana mood. Says everyone's dead *laissez-faire*, you know.

Tania   Did you get laid?

Steph   *Naturellement.*

Wendy   Well, let's face it, when did Steph never get laid?

Steph   Thursday night, Wend, why?

Wendy   You're slipping.

Steph   Well, warn me if I'm reaching your level.

Lee   Should I go and have a look at the food?

Wendy   No, I'll do it. (*Exits.*)

Tania   I'm starving.

Roy   Are you on a diet?

Tania   Cheeky bastard, no!

Roy   Oh, sorry.

Nick   She's constantly on a diet.

Tania   Nobody's interested, Nick.

Nick   You've just bought that video!

Roy   Ah, which one?

Tania   Nick!

Nick   'Linda Robson's Light As A Feather.'

Roy   Oh, I've got that, it's brilliant, isn't it?

Nick   I was quite impressed actually, it's like, she's bringing nutrition to the people.

Steph Really?

Nick Yeah.

Steph Great.

Nick No, seriously.

Tania He's being serious.

Roy Eh, Nick, just think, one day you might be doing your own diet video.

Tania Called 'Nick East's ballooned since RADA'. He has, you know, he's put on so much weight.

Roy Is that your surname? East?

Nick My real name's Ross, so I had to change it for Equity's purposes.

Roy Where d'you get East from? Your mam's side?

Nick No, my first job was *Eastenders*. I took it from that.

Steph Good job it wasn't *Country Practice*.

Roy Who were you in *Eastenders*?

Nick Robbie McFee.

Roy Who was he?

Nick I was drunk and abusive in the Queen Vic.

Steph Fifteen minutes to go.

Roy (*to* **Nick**) Are you fat?

Nick I've been thinner. I lost two stone for a part last year.

Roy Which part?

Nick It was set in a hospice.

Roy Oh, was that that thing about the fella who was dying and his dream was to buy his wife an engagement ring so he went on the rob and ended up in jail? She was in it, her off *Desmond's*, ah, it was great that!

Nick   No, this was called 'Heartbreak Holiday'. It was a . . . fringe production.

Lee (*proudly*)   The *Jewish Chronicle* said he was really good at misery.

Roy   Why are they called hospices?

Steph   Can we get into Eurovision mood please? If it's not too much to ask? I mean, that is the reason why we are all here. Thank you.

Roy   Me Uncle Albert were put in a hospice. I remember me mam saying, 'Your Uncle Albert's gone in a hospice.' I thought it were just a trendy way o' saying hospital.

Pause.

So when me mam went into hospital for her women's operation I told me teacher me mum'd gone in a hospice. She let me draw all afternoon. Everyone else was doing maths.

Pause.

There was bloody murder when she came to sports day.

Lee *has rushed out to the bedroom.*

Roy   I wonder if it's Greek, meaning 'A place you go to die'.

Steph   That's not hospice, that's Bury St Edmunds.

Nick   I'm . . . (*Gets up to follow* **Lee**.)

Tania (*to* **Nick**)   Leave him, Blobs.

Nick   I better . . .

Tania (*to* **Nick**)   He might wanna be on his own.

Nick   I'll check.

Nick *exits.*

Tania   Can't be easy, can it? If this time o'year holds big memories and that.

Steph   I believe Nick's been a tower of strength.

Tania   Yeah, well, he's a man's man.

Steph   Oh, yeah?

Tania (*tuts*)   Him and Lee have always been close.

Steph   Inseparable.

Tania   Mike was my mate right from school. Nick and Lee were our partners. They formed a special bond.

Roy   Like footballers' wives.

Tania   Nick aint queer, Steph.

Steph   I never said he was.

Tania (*getting up*)   Not tonight, no. (*She goes towards the kitchen.*) Need hand, Wend?

Wendy (*off*)   Please!

Tania *exits to kitchen, leaving door open.* **Steph** *and* **Roy** *are left on their own.*

Steph   And then there were two.

Roy   Two what?

Steph   Eurovision fans.

Roy   Did I . . . ?

Pause.

I did, didn't I. Oh, God, I'm always saying the wrong thing. All the time. I get nervous see. (*Starts to cry.*)

Steph *gets out of his seat and goes and sits next to* **Roy.**

Steph   Oh now, Roy, m'darling. Roy Roy Roy Roy Roy. What are we gonna do with you?

Roy   Nothing.

Steph   Now, Roy, come on. Unburden those humungous woes please. (*Puts his arm round him.*)

Roy   Get off.

Steph   I know how it feels you know, to feel you can't do a thing right. Every time I try and get close to Lee, Nick gets in the way.

Roy *gets up.*

Steph   Where you going?

Roy   Nowhere.

Roy *goes and stands on the balcony.*

Steph   Well, let . . .

Roy   You stay right there I'm all right.

Roy *has his back to us, leaning over the railings looking out, possibly crying.* **Steph** *is left alone on the sofa. There is a knock at the door,* **Steph** *goes and answers it. It's* **Norman**.

Norman   Hiya, I'm Norman.

Steph   Hi there.

Norman   I'm from upstairs. Well. I'm from Liverpool really, but I live upstairs. I was just wondering if the chair was all right.

Steph   It's great actually, now thank you so much for making tonight a possibility bumwise.

Norman   God, where is everyone? Have they all done a runner?

Steph   Just . . . powdering their various noses. And . . . any other body part you care to mention. Only joking, yep?

Norman   Oh well, just thought I'd check.

Steph   Well, it's nice to know that manners are alive and well and living in Kentish Town actually, Norman.

Norman   Sad time o'the year the Eurovision, isn't it?

Steph   Well . . .

Norman   Don't worry he told me everything. And I mean everything. Thought I'd pop down now coz I know it's starting soon.

Nick *enters from the bedroom. He collects his and* **Lee**'s *glasses.*

Steph   What?

Norman   The contest. (*To* **Nick**.) Hiya.

Nick   Hi. Just taking these through to the bedroom.

Steph   Everything hunky-dory with Lee in there, Nick?

Nick   Nearly. You don't know where he keeps his hankies, do you?

Steph   No.

Nick   It's all right, I'll get some toilet paper.

Nick *exits to bedroom.*

Norman   God, Richard Gere or what?

Steph   Actually . . .

Norman   Been round an awful lot lately that one, you know. Still, if they've made it to the bedroom tonight of all nights, all I can say is about time too. I know they haven't been at it yet coz me floorboards are like that. (*Shows just how thin they are with his finger and thumb.*) Toilet paper eh? I prefer a hot towel meself. Best be getting back. Ah, it was nice to meet yer anyway.

Steph   I'm Steph incidentally.

Norman (*shaking his hand*)   That's an unusual surname. Only kidding yer.

Steph   I hope we meet again, Norman.

Norman   Oh, you can come up any time, you know. I'm the youngest of twelve, I'm used to having people round me.

Steph   I might just have to do that. Run along now.

Norman   Trar.

Steph   Ciao for now.

Norman *goes.* **Steph** *goes to the kitchen door.*

Steph   Okay in there, girls, are we?

Wendy (*off*)   Fine!

The kitchen door slams shut in **Steph**'s *face. He goes towards the balcony.*

Steph   Roy.

Pause.

You've done nothing wrong, you know. If Lee can't bear to hear the word hospice then that's his lookout.

Pause.

I'm all on my ownsome lonesome in here actually, Roy.

Pause.

Roy, this is Steph. Your old buddy.

Roy   Buddy off.

Roy *closes the balcony door and goes back and leans on the railings.* **Steph** *sits down and has a swig of his drink. He pours himself another Bucks Fizz. He reads his scoring card. He looks at his watch. He gets up and goes to the television set. He switches it on. Nothing. He bangs on it. Nothing. He hits it again. Nothing. He checks it is plugged in. It is. He switches it off then on again. Nothing. This time he slaps it in annoyance. A small explosion is heard inside the TV. He looks horrified. Another small explosion. Terror. He looks around. He switches the telly on and off. Nothing. It's dead. He retreats to his chair and sits uneasily looking round at the various doors. He looks at his watch. He gets the phone off the floor and dials a number.*

Steph (*on phone*)   Hello, Billy. Steph. Hi. What you up to then? Well, I was just sitting in at home and, you know, having bumped into you at Sainsbury's last night I thought, 'I know what. I'll give Billy a ring.' Not going to Lee's tonight? No, me neither. It's a bit awkward, isn't it? Yep. Yep. I mean, between you and me, he tends to get just a little too over emotional for my liking, so. No. No. No, I didn't go whole hog for the brain tumour story either. I mean it's obvious, isn't it? And I mean, we both saw the state he got into on World Aids Day. I mean it's not everyone who sticks a red ribbon on their hatchback. Mm. So. What you up to tonight? Right. Is that voices I can hear in the background? Oh. Must be my party line. Oh, is it? Oh, right, well, I better get the telly on, hadn't I? Oh, there's my doorbell, must go. I've got a couple of friends round from the London Nude Swimmers so. Okay, Billy. You too. Fingers crossed for Love City Groove eh? Yeah. Ciao for now. Bye. Bye.

He puts the phone down. He goes in his bumbag for a business card. He gets it out, he picks the phone up again and dials the number from the card.

Hi, Victor? Steph. Hi. Remember when we played that trick on your ex? That's right, that's the one. Well, I need you to do it for me now. Yeah. To Billy's house. Well, I can't coz I'm round at Lee's. You got Billy's address? Great. Remember, different cab company each time. Get your Yellow Pages out. Okay, Victor. Let your fingers do the walking. Love you for it. Yeah. Bye.

He puts the phone down. He doesn't know what to do. He switches the TV off then runs off to the hall and shuts the door. At the same time the kitchen door opens and **Wendy** *enters with a plate of garlic bread, she comes in and puts it on the coffee-table.* **Tania** *follows with a selection of dips.* **Wendy** *stands looking at her. It's important that they are positioned so neither of them can see* **Roy** *on the balcony.*

Tania   Where is everyone? (*Beat.*) What?

Wendy   I dare you.

Tania   What?

Wendy   Here.

Tania   Are you bleeding mad?

Wendy   I think I must be.

Tania   You are, you're a bleeding nutter.

Tania *moves towards* **Wendy***. They giggle then kiss.* **Tania** *backs off.*

Tania   Wend.

Wendy   I know.

Tania   Shut up.

Wendy (*nodding towards kitchen*)   Crudités.

They go off to the kitchen. **Roy** *comes back in to get a cigarette. He takes one of* **Steph**'s*, lights it, and returns to the balcony, shutting the door behind him. He leans agains the railing, looking down, his back to the lounge.* **Tania** *and* **Wendy** *enter again with trays of sliced vegetables.*

Wendy   They must all be in with Lee. Probably having an orgy.

She opens the door to the hall.

Why don't we?

Tania   No.

Wendy   No?

Tania   No.

Wendy   (*advancing towards her*)   No?

Tania   (*whispered but insistent*)   NO!

Wendy   You know what they say about women who say no.

Tania   No?

Wendy   No. Neither do I.

They kiss again. **Roy** *wipes his eyes and turns round to come back in. He sees* **Wendy** *and* **Tania** *kissing. He is gobsmacked. His jaw drops and the cigarette falls to the ground. Immediately it ignites the spilt petrol and a modest fire begins to burn on the balcony.* **Wendy** *and* **Tania** *are oblivious to this.* **Tania** *stops the snog.*

Tania   No.

Wendy   Okay.

Tania   No. Kitchen.

They hurry off to the kitchen and close the door. The fire is getting bigger. **Roy** *can't get back into the flat because the fire is blocking his way. He screams.* **Nick** *enters with his drink from the bedroom.*

Roy   (*from balcony*)   Shit! Shit! Shit! Shit! (*Sees* **Nick**.) Tango! Tango!!

Nick   Shit!

Nick *gets some damp tops from the clothes-horse. He opens the balcony door and slaps the fire out with the tops, then jumps up and down on it. Soon the fire is out.* **Nick** *stands in the lounge with the tops and* **Roy** *stays on the balcony.*

Roy   I'm sorry. I forgot your name.

Nick   Are you okay?

Roy   Yeah.

Nick   What the fucking hell happened, man?

Roy I dropped a ciggie.

Nick   In that? Jesus Christ, come in.

Roy Can't.

Nick What?

Roy I can't.

Nick   Eh?

Roy I've wet meself.

Nick   I'll get a cloth from the kitchen.

Roy No! No!

Nick Well . . . I'll get some trousers from Lee.

Roy Please.

Nick What?

Roy Don't tell anyone I went on the balcony. It's Lee, see. He told me not to. He didn't want anyone on here. You mustn't tell anyone I was here not even your wife.

Nick Partner.

Roy Tania, don't tell her, promise?

Nick Well . . .

Roy It'd mean a lot to me. I loved the Tango advert. And . . . I haven't told you this before but you were belting in that *Bill* episode.

Nick Which one?

Roy All of 'em. I saw 'em all. Please. I'm a kleptomaniac.

Nick   Sorry?

Roy I'm addicted to setting fire to things. You understand. You're having treatment. Please. Our secret.

Nick   Okay.

Roy I really appreciate this.

Nick   Come in.

Roy   Tar.

Roy *comes in off the balcony. He has a wet patch down one of the legs of his jeans, emanating from his crotch.*

Nick   I didn't realise you erm, had followed my career so closely. I mean, the core of my work's been theatre but. Well. What can I say?

Roy   Mm.

Nick   I appreciate you holding back. I get it a lot. You know.

Roy   Adoration?

Nick   Well.

Roy   I'm not surprised.

Nick   Makes a refreshing change when someone . . . Hey, thanks.

He hugs **Roy**.

Roy   Close the door.

Nick   What? Oh right.

Nick *shuts the balcony door.*

Roy   He won't notice for ages, he never goes out there. (*Looks at his trousers.*) Oh, God, does it show?

Nick   Well. It's nothing to be embarrassed about, you're amongst friends. Where's Steph?

Roy   Dunno. I'll soak them. In the bathroom. You look hungry. Have something to eat. Don't, whatever you do, go in the kitchen.

Nick   Why not?

Roy   Coz Wendy's . . . talking to Tania about the pins in her knee. I think it's like counselling.

Nick   Tania? Counselling?

Roy   Have you noticed they've been spending time together lately?

Nick   No, her mum's been ill. Emphysema.

Roy   Oh. Well, that's what's happening now. And treatment's like, confidential. Isn't it?

Nick   Strictly.

Roy   Start the food off, go on.

Nick   Right. You okay?

Roy   Yeah. Are you gay?

Nick   No.

Roy   No, I didn't think you were. I can spot it a mile off.

Nick *sits to eat*.

Roy   So you're not shagging Lee or owt?

Nick   Roy, mate, listen.

Roy   I don't mind. I won't tell anyone.

Nick   Roy!! For fuck's sake! I'm straight. I wish I wasn't half the time, you guys can get it when you want.

Roy   And you're not in an open relationship?

Nick   Roy. You're a nice lad. Handsome. But threesomes aint in our line, mate.

Roy   I'll put these in to soak in the bathroom.

Lee *enters*.

Roy (*to* **Lee**)   What do you want?!

Lee   Food!

Roy   Sorry. I've spilt Bucks Fizz down me jeans, I'm gonna soak 'em in the bathroom.

Lee (*sees stain*)   Oh no! (*Realises.*) Steph's in there.

Roy   Where?

Lee   In the bathroom.

Roy   Right.

Lee   Look if you stick them in the washer on an economy wash they can be dry by the end of the contest. I've got a drier.

Lee *heads to the kitchen.*

Roy   No!!

Lee (*stops*)   You what?

Roy   They're handwash only.

Lee   They're 501s, aren't they?

Roy   No! Oh . . .

Roy *bursts out crying.*

Lee   Oh, Roy, love eh? Eh? (*Goes to him.*) It's only a bit of Bucks Fizz. (*Wipes his hand on* **Roy**'s *wet patch and then licks his finger.*) Mm? (*He hugs* **Roy**.)

Roy   It's not that.

Lee   Well, what is it?

Roy   Erm . . .

Tania *and* **Wendy** *enter from the kitchen.*

Nick   Everything okay, ladies?

Wendy   Fine.

Tania (*to* **Nick**)   Why aren't you eating?

Nick   I am.

Wendy   Oh, Roy, puppy, what's up?

Roy   Nothing.

Tania   Eeh! What've you spilt down your strides, Roy?

Roy   Nothing.

Wendy   Roy, what is it?

Roy   Bucks Fizz.

Wendy   No. What's the matter?

Lee   Eh?

Nick   I think I know.

Tania   Yeah, well, you think you know everything, duntcha?

Roy   Tania!!

Tania   What?!

Roy   Don't have a go at him!

Tania   Do what? And just who d'you think you're talking to eh?

Nick   Tania!

Tania   I am not having him talk to me like that!

Lee   He's upset.

Nick   Actually, if you must know.

Tania   What?

Lee
Wendy}   What?

Nick (*beat*)   His . . . his dog died this afternoon.

Steph *enters from the bathroom.*

Steph   Ooh, had a right lamppost to get rid of there. Beautiful. Just about time, isn't it? Stick the telly on, Nick.

Pause.

Nick   Isn't that right, Roy?

Roy   Mm.

Lee   I didn't know you had a dog, Roy.

Roy   I only got her this morning.

Wendy   Oh, Roy, how did she die?

Nick   Run down. On her first walk.

Lee   Come and sit down, Roy.

Wendy   Yeah, oh, baby. Get him a brandy, Lee.

Roy   Oh, yeah, I need a drink.

Lee *goes into the kitchen.* **Roy** *ends up wedged between* **Tania** *and* **Wendy** *on the couch.*

Steph   Nick? Stick telly on. I'm hopeless with them old contraptions.

Tania   This boy's just lost his dog.

Steph   Have you got a dog, Roy?

Tania   Not any more, obviously.

Wendy   What was her name?

Roy   Dyke ... andra.

Steph   I love it!

Roy   Dykandra.

Lee *enters with a bottle of brandy and a glass. He starts pouring one for* **Roy** *on the coffee-table.*

Nick   Dykandra.

Tania   What sort was she?

Roy   Lesbian.

Lee   What?

Nick   It was a very special dog. Female. And attracted only to other bitches.

Steph   Well, she'd be better off dead.

Roy   We're going to miss the opening.

Wendy   Oh, Nick, you're nearest.

Lee   I'll do it, it's a bit temperamental.

Wendy (*to* **Roy**)   Oh, you poor baby.

Roy *sips the brandy as* **Lee** *switches the television on. He messes around with the switches on it till his next line.*

Roy   I'm all right. I think it's the excitement of tonight. And ... I'll be all right when the contest's on.

Wendy   Can you eat something?

Steph I'm ravenous actually.

Tania (*to* **Roy**) Try and eat something, mate. Wend's gone to a lot of trouble with that.

Lee I don't believe it.

Nick What?

Lee I was right.

Tania What?

Lee He *is* here.

Steph Who?

Lee Michael.

Wendy Lee?

Nick Lee. Is it plugged in?

Lee He doesn't want me to see it. He doesn't want me to enjoy it without him.

Steph You're not trying to tell me the telly's broken down, are you?

Roy What?

Nick Lee, we've talked about this.

Lee Haven't we just.

Nick You said.

Lee Yeah.

Nick What did you say?

Tania Nick?

Nick You said . . . you were going to move forwards.

Lee (*joining in*) Move forwards. (*Clears his throat.*) Move forwards and see it through. I'm going to watch it. I'm going to fucking well watch it! But how can I when the telly's buggered?

Roy It's not, is it?

Tania I'll phone Billy. We can all go over to his.

Steph   Now *that* is the most ridiculous thing I've ever heard in my life!

Roy   Why is it?

Steph (*to* **Lee**)   After the way he's treated you? Snubbed you? On your special night?

Wendy   Steph's got a point.

Steph   You and Michael threw the best Eurovision parties around. But now Michael's gone Billy can't even bring himself to come. Don't do it, Lee.

Roy   We were all invited.

Steph (*not impressed*)   Were we?!

Wendy   Steph's right.

Steph   Well, there's a first.

Lee   How am I going to watch it?!

Wendy   Isn't it on Radio Two?

Lee
Roy   } IT'S NOT THE SAME!!!
Steph

Tania   She's only trying to help.

Wendy   Well, there's only one thing for it.

A knock at the door suddenly. **Steph** *gets it. All eyes on the door. It's* **Norman**.

Norman (*peering in*)   Have I called at a bad time?

They all look at each other.

Blackout.

In the blackout the Eurovision theme music begins to play.

Act Two

Lights up on **Wendy** *and* **Tania** *putting the food from the coffee-table onto trays to be carried upstairs.*

Wendy We could say we're going to the pub.

Tania Ssh. (*Nods in the direction of the main door.*) Nick.

Wendy (*loudly, deliberately*) I don't know whether I fancy this Eurovision lark. Don't want to come to the pub, do you, Tania?

Pause.

Tania (*quietly*) He's going through a hard time. I know I take the piss but . . .

Pause. **Tania** *continues to fill her tray.* **Wendy** *watches her, hurt. Just then* **Norman** *enters from the hall.*

Norman Oh, aren't yous marvellous?

He picks up his armchair.

I think we'll be wanting this, don't you?

Tania Yeah.

Tania *exits hurriedly with her tray.*

Norman You know where it is, don't yer?

Wendy Yeah. Thanks.

Wendy *hurries out.* **Norman** *puts the armchair down, looks at photo of* Michael.

Norman Ah, God love him.

Goes to **Tania**'s *handbag, looks in and sniffs it. He puts it on his shoulder and goes to the mirror.*

Well, tonight, Matthew, I'm going to be . . . Kiki Dee.

Waves to mirror. Puts bag down. Taps coffee-table.

(*To chair.*) That's glass.

Sits on sofa.

(*To one chair.*) I know. (*To other chair.*) I know. I said to the fella I want from there to there covered in pine. Well, I can afford it, you know. (*Up, to the kitchen doors.*) This is the saloon bar effect.

A toilet flushes off and **Nick** *enters.* **Norman** *sees him.*

Norman   He's got some lovely bits, hasn't he?

Nick   What? Yeah. Got it really homely.

Norman   Sort of place you could envisage yourself living in, is it?

Nick   Well. It's central.

Norman   I'm not being lesbophobic or nothing, but them two are really pretty.

Nick   Sorry?

Norman   Them lesbians.

Nick   Actually they're both straight.

Norman   Oh, well, I was right then, wasn't I?

Roy *enters from hall. He wears a towel round his waist instead of jeans.*

Nick   Oright, Roy?

Norman (*laughs*)   God! Fancy me thinking they were lesbians! God, I can't get over that, can you? Aray I'll see you upstairs then, yeah?

Norman *picks up his armchair and exits.* **Roy** *stands looking sheepish.*

Nick   Roy?

Roy   Erm.

Nick   What's up?

Roy   Nothing.

Nick   I hope you're not embarrassed that I know.

Roy   Know what?

Nick   What happened.

Roy When?

Nick Look if it's any consolation, I shat myself on stage once.

Roy What?

Nick Admittedly I had gastroenteritis but, hey, the show must go on. It was a three-hander Julius Caesar. We were all in togas, so I got stage management – they're these guys who, kind of, well, they . . . do stuff, set the props, prompt your lines. Not that they had to prompt me – I was off the book at the read through . . . unlike Derek. Anyway, yeah, I got them to make me a nappy out of towels and masking tape. Nobody knew. But I did. And, Christ, did I feel humiliated.

Roy *stands up and heads for the hall.* **Tania** *enters.*

Nick Where you going?

Roy Toilet. I need an E.

Nick An E?

Roy I brought two for later. I'm gonna take one now.

Nick Right.

Roy I've got to.

He exits. **Nick** *sits down on the settee and rests his head in his hands, thinking.*

Tania You coming up or what?

Nick Yeah, I'll be up in a sec.

Tania I mean, you know, you drag me over for some piece of shit and then . . .

Nick I did *not* drag you over. Christ! I couldn't believe you said you'd come.

Tania I'm not totally heartless, you know. Mike was my mate!

Nick It's the first time in fucking ages you haven't had to go running off to bloody Islington every five minutes.

Tania My mum aint well!

Nick Yeah, well, I wish she'd save us all the hassle and die now.

Pause.

Tania   Well, I'm sorry to disappoint you, Nicholarse, but she happens to be making a recovery.

Nick   Oh, maybe I'll get to see you once in a blue moon.

Tania   I can't help it if me mum's ill.

Nick   Convenient, isn't it?

Tania   What?

Nick   That she gets ill all of a sudden.

Tania   She's been up and down for years, you know that.

Nick   Oh, do I?

Tania   You think I'm making it up?

Pause.

You are gonna regret you even thought that, you cunt. I want an apology. And I aint moving one cell till I get one.

Roy *enters from the bathroom, relaxed.*

Roy   Where are they up to?

Tania   Sorry but I can't see through ceilings.

Roy   God, imagine what it'd be like to see through ceilings.

Nick   Roy ... er ...

Tania (*to* **Nick**)   I'm waiting.

Roy   I best get up.

Roy *exits.*

Tania   You know what you do? You make me wanna heave. If I was anorexic I wouldn't waste me time with laxatives or sticking knitting needles down me throat, I'd just take one look at you.

Nick   I'm sorry.

Tania   You wanna be glad you've got me. I'm a fucking result.

Tania *pours herself a drink and lights herself a cigarette.*

Nick   It's all this freedom. Not working. My mind works overtime.

Tania   You haven't got a mind. Look at you. You're a waste of space. I'd be better off having an affair. Don't look at me like that, all doey-eyed, you said it.

Nick   I didn't.

Tania   What do I do then? If I aint visiting my mum?

Nick (*shrugs*)   Got a fancy man?

Tania   A fancy man. I've already got a fancy man. Very fancy. Fancies himself as a fucking star. And I have to put up with his fancy ways, dunn'I? No. I don't. And won't. Grow up, Nick.

Nick   I wouldn't blame you. I'm not much cop to live with at the moment.

Tania   You never were, darling.

Nick   Your mum can't stand the sight of me, I can't stand the thought of her. Ideal excuse. See? Got it all worked out. (*It's obvious he doesn't believe this.*)

Tania   D'you know what you are? You're one sad bastard. You don't even believe that.

Nick   I think I might be depressed.

Tania   Oi! There's somebody else in the room! Jesus. Even when you're accusing me of sleeping around, it's gotta get back to you!

Nick   It's this freedom thing.

Tania   Is someone paying you to say that word?

Nick   I have all this time to myself to think the stupidest things. To hatch the stupidest schemes.

Tania   Well, here's a little scheme for you to hatch. You'll like this one. You get on the blower, you hire a removal van and you get out sharpish. Like that one, do ya? Thought you would. You're spoilt. God help the poor mug who gets you next.

Nick   Fine I'll move out.

Tania (*rubs hands together*)   Excellent. A result.

Nick   I can't remember the last time you said you loved me.

Tania   Me neither, shame that.

She goes to the door.

(*Sarcastic.*) I love you. How's that?

Nick   You'd make a crap actor.

Tania   You *are* a crap actor.

Tania *exits to go upstairs.* **Nick** *is left on his own. He begins to recite a speech from the last play he was in.*

Nick   Why is my life such a mess? In tatters? Shattered like a piece of broken glass you take your fist to. Clenched first, broken wrist, Rizla papers torn to shreds. Shredded beds of nothingness. I am a mess. Guess. Bless this House. I no longer live here. The psychic spines of broken glass that pierce this very skin, but where do I begin to even lick the wounds you cause me?

Lee *enters behind him.*

Nick (*continues*)   I loved you once. I loved you all. But fall is the season of distrust. I must. I must. I must. Depart. (*Sees* **Lee**.) 'Psychodrama' by Chuck Finnegan.

Lee   Don't let me stop you.

Nick   I think it's all over with me and Tania. I'm being as horrible as is humanly possible.

Lee   I think Jeffrey Dahmer pipped you to the post on that one. (*Tuts.*) Surely it's not irretrievable.

Nick   Christ, Lee, why aren't I gay?

Lee (*shrugs*)   Too close an association with your father in your pre-school years?

Nick   We'd make a great team.

Lee   Yeah, but the sex'd be pretty lousy.

Nick   I'm a quick learner.

Lee   But would your heart be in it?

Nick   Me arse would! (*More serious.*) I envy you bastards.

Lee   I think it's a case of the grass is always greener, dear.

Nick   Shit. I'm sorry. See? I can say sorry to you at the drop of a hat and mean it, but Tania?

Lee   D'you love her?

Nick   I'm used to her.

Lee   Isn't that the same thing?

Nick   No.

Lee   No.

Nick   I dunno.

Lee   Where would you go?

Nick   I don't know.

Pause.

Lee   You could always come here you know.

Pause.

Go up and talk to her.

Nick   And tell her what?

Lee   I don't know.

Nick   I can't talk to her like I can talk to you.

Lee   Get up there and salvage it, Nick.

Nick   Right.

Lee   If you want to.

Nick   Yeah. I do.

Lee   Well, hurry up.

Nick   You're a fucking good mate, Lee.

Lee   Everything's easier with mates.

Nick   You are.

Lee   Go on, you're beginning to sound like someone from *The Wonder Years*.

Nick   That's an excellent show.

Nick *exits.* **Lee** *moves to the stereo and puts on a CD of Annie Lennox singing 'Why'. He looks at the CD cover. He fights tears. He takes the photo of Michael off the wall and holds it to him. He sits on the sofa and hugs the photo to him. On the line 'This boat is sinking',* **Steph** *enters, he sees* **Lee** *sitting on the sofa fighting tears.* **Steph** *tries to stop* **Norman** *entering but he does.* **Steph** *pushes* **Norman** *out of the room then re-enters.* **Steph** *turns the sound down.* **Lee** *looks round.*

Steph   Annie Lennox? Sacrilege tonight, dear.

Lee *turns the sound down a bit.*

Lee   Sometimes we had taste. It wasn't all tack. I used to play this whenever . . . I always opened my big mouth, then he'd open his, then silence. It was easier to say sorry by playing this, than actually working up the courage to . . . And now it's . . . He'd be standing there, where you are. I'd put this on. And there'd be no need to talk.

He gets up, snaps the stereo off, then sits down again.

I don't know whether to phone Billy. We had a row in Sainsbury's last night. Frozen foods. When I saw him reach in that freezer and bring out a party-bag of mini sausage rolls I just saw red.

'He had a brain tumour you stupid soft prick!' I yelled. 'He had a fucking brain tumour!'

Maybe it would have been easier if he had had AIDS. We certainly wouldn't have hidden it. Well, you don't, do you? But oh no that's not good enough for the likes of Billy. It couldn't possibly have been a brain tumour. 'He lost three stone!' he yelled at me. God, he was on a fucking diet, wasn't he? He was on a diet because I didn't fancy him with a beer gut and a bit of a double chin! If he'd had AIDS I'd've been prepared for it . . . this . . . and been able to say . . . I should phone Billy. I hit him round the head with a frozen chicken.

Pause.

I said some terrible things. Personal. He must think I hate him.
My parting retort was, 'I'll get my own back on you!'

Pause.

We're okay with AIDS. We expect AIDS. We don't expect a
brain tumour. I thought he'd gone off me coz it was always 'Not
now Lee I've got a headache.' I should phone Billy.

Steph   Don't phone Billy. He's not worth it. I wouldn't piss on
him if he begged me. I'd piss on you. If you asked nicely.

Lee   You mad bastard.

Steph   Well . . . in the immortal words of Teach-In, seventy-
five,

> 'When you're feeling all right,
> Everything is uptight,
> Try to sing a song that goes
> Ding, Ding a Dong.

> And the world is sunny,
> Everyone is funny,
> When they sing a song
> That goes Ding Dang Dong.'

Lee   Sometimes the Dutch put it so much better than we ever
could.

Steph   I feel a bit silly now.

Lee   What?

Steph   No, it's nothing.

Lee   What?

Steph   Well . . .

Lee   Steph?

Steph   Can I borrow your bedroom for five minutes? No
longer, I promise.

Pause.

It's Norman. He's er . . .

Lee   You what?

Steph   Well, Nick and Tania are in his bedroom and Love City Groove are on shortly. I won't be long, I promise. We'll clean up after ourselves.

Pause.

I never once doubted the brain tumour story.

Lee   It wasn't a story.

Steph   Exactly.

Lee (*nods*)   Yeah. Go'ed.

Steph *is delighted.*

Steph   You know, I think he's rather sexy, in a Chaucerian sort o'way. (*Calls.*) Norman?!

Norman *enters sheepishly.*

Steph   Now the very marvellous Lee has kindly given his permission for us two to use his boudoir. Say thank you, you ungrateful little slut!

Norman   Thanks, Lee. It's dead kind o' you, y'know. No, it is.

Steph (*conspiratorially to* **Lee**)   Don't have a spare table-tennis bat knocking about, do you?

Lee   No. There's a fish server in the kitchen.

Steph   Stainless steel? (**Lee** *nods.*) Cheers m'darling. (*Making his way to kitchen, hollers at* **Norman**.) And you can get in the bedroom!

Steph *exits to the kitchen.* **Lee** *picks up the phone. He rings a number, waits, then puts the phone down.* **Steph** *returns with a stainless-steel fish server.*

Lee   Engaged.

Steph *goes in his bumbag and gets the handcuffs out.*

Steph   Have you got a radio through there?

Lee Yeah.

Steph What's its Radio Two reception like?

Lee Fine.

Steph Good.

Steph *exits with the fish server and handcuffs. Presently* **Roy** *ambles in.*

Roy Are my pupils dilated?

Lee (*looks at his eyes*) No.

Roy I'll kill that dealer.

He gets a wrap of coke out of his pocket and a credit card out of his wallet and starts chopping up some coke on the glass coffee-table.

Didn't feel I could do it in front of Wendy. She'd probably think I had a drug problem.

Lee Is Wend on her own?

Roy Yeah. D'you want some?

Lee *shakes his head.*

Roy D'you think I've got a drug problem?

Lee Do you?

Roy Not sure. I hope not. (*Slicing it into a line now.*) I . . . only . . . do it . . . of an evening. I mean, it's not like I . . . wake up of a morning and . . . neck three Es. It's just . . . I've gotta stop it. It's no wonder . . . I'm always so skint. (*He gets a twenty-pound note out of his wallet and rolls it up.*) Sure you don't want any?

Lee Sod it, why not.

Roy You take first half. You'll feel better for that.

Lee (*sticking the note up his nose*) I don't think you've got a problem. (*Snorts half the line.*)

Roy No, neither do I. (*Snorts the other half.*)

Lee I better get up and check on Wendy. And the contest.

Roy You do that.

Lee   I will. (*At the door now.*) I was sorry to hear about your dog.

Roy   So was I.

Lee *exits.* **Roy** *slices up a second line then snorts it. As he is cleaning up after himself.* **Steph** *comes in with the fish server and heads for the kitchen.*

Steph   Don't want a go, do you?

Roy   No, tar.

Steph   Fair enough.

Steph *exits to kitchen. He returns carrying a spiky wooden spaghetti server.*

Roy   Steph, you know Wendy?

Steph   Unfortunately.

Roy   Has she ever had a fella?

Steph   A guy from Stevenage, didn't last. Knocked her about a bit, sensible man.

Roy   Don't be horrible, you.

Steph   Why do you ask, m'darling?

Roy   D'you ever get the feeling she's dykey?

Steph   Well, put it this way, if she hasn't got k.d. lang in her CD collection I'd be pretty fucking surprised.

Roy   No, but do you?

Steph   I don't think so. Why?

Roy   Oh, nothing really.

Steph   Right.

Roy   It's just that I saw her snog the golly off Tania before and I just put two and . . . (*Stops himself.*)

Pause.

I didn't really, that were a joke.

Steph   Was it?

Roy   I think I'm coming up on me E.

Steph   Roy?

Roy *starts stretching his arms in the air like he is waking up. The Ecstasy he took earlier is beginning to take effect. He rolls his head round.*

Roy   In here. Bold as daylight. Don't tell no one.

Steph   You really saw . . . no! No!!

Steph *sits down, mulling this over.* **Roy** *doesn't really take much care with what he says now as he is enjoying his ecstatic state.*

Roy   You mustn't tell anybody. Least of all Lee. I mean. Ah, wow, I feel great. Do you feel great? Oh, I feel fab! Oh, I wanno stretch out and, oh, this is really nice. Ah, Steph, will you rub me head?

Steph *gets up, stands behind* **Roy** *and rubs his head for him.*

Roy   Oh, that's so good. That is just, ah, wow.

Steph   Wendy and . . . It's all beginning to make sense now.

Roy   I know it's fab, isn't it?

Steph   I don't believe . . .

Roy   You haven't taken an E, have you?

Steph   What would Michael say?

Roy   I don't think he ever did it, did he?

Steph   What?

Roy   E!

Steph   They've been . . . all o'them . . . bloody hell, Roy. D'you realise what this means?

The phone rings. **Steph** *exits for the bedroom in a daze.* **Roy** *slowly goes to the phone, his eyes rolling and answers it lying on the foor. Rolling around.*

Roy   Hello? Hello? No, it's Roy. Do I sound like Lee? I didn't think I did. Do I sound like I'm on helium? Good, it's embarrassing when I get like that. Don't shout. Who is it? Billy, hiya! Oh, Billy, don't shout, there's no need to shout. Okay I'll get him. Billy, I don't know whether I've told you this before but I love you. I think you're fab. Ah don't shout.

Roy *gets up and goes to the door. He softly calls out.*

Roy   Lee! Lee, it's Billy!

Steph *comes out from the bedroom and into the lounge with the pasta server.*

Steph   Did you just say Billy?

Roy   Yeah. He's shouting. Why's he shouting?

Steph (*shouts*)   Lee!! Lee!!

Roy   Will you rub me head again?

Steph   Couch.

Roy *sits on the couch,* **Steph** *rubs his head.* **Roy** *is in ecstasy.* **Lee** *enters.*

Lee   What?

Steph   Billy on the phone. Seems to be getting a tad terse.

Lee   Billy?

He goes to the phone. He sits to speak.

Hiya, Billy. Bill, do you have to . . . (*Shouts.*) Bill, I'm not deaf!! (*More calm.*) You cheeky get, as if I'd do a thing like that. Billy! Billy! Now hang on a minute! (*Pause.* **Lee** *puts the phone down.*) The cheeky bastard. He's had taxis coming every five minutes and he's tryina make out I ordered them! I'll fucking . . . says he's gonna get his own back.

Steph   Maybe you did do it, Lee.

Lee   What?

Steph   Maybe you did.

Lee   Steph . . . you've been here all night, you'd've seen.

Steph   Well, I seem to recall you saying earlier you'd seen Billy in Sainsbury's and said you'd get your own back.

Lee   I wouldn't do a thing like that.

Steph   Wouldn't you? You're probably right. What would I know?

Lee   You should know that's not my style. Where's Norman?

Steph   Fuck him, where's Nick?

Lee   Nick's talking to Tania. Isn't he?

Steph   What are they talking about?

Lee   What's the matter, Steph?

Steph   We're your mates. Don't you think if you've got something to tell us, we've got a right to know? Out of common courtesy. Manners.

Lee   Y'what? Like what?

Steph   Lee, we know what's going on.

Lee   What's going on?

Roy   Yeah, what's going on?

Steph   I'm going home.

Steph *heads for the door.*

Lee   What? Steph, what's the matter?

Steph   I'm not jealous.

Lee *stops him from leaving the room, grabbing his arm.*

Lee   Steph?

Steph   Do I have to spell it out to you?

Lee   Well, I wouldn't mind. Have I done something to upset you?

Steph   No.

Lee   What then?

Steph   I worry about your head, Lee. You're so caught up in 'doing the right thing'. The man of principle. When all along you're just a bloody great hypocrite.

Lee   How come?

Roy   Rub me head.

Lee   I dunno what the fuck you're talking about, Steph!

Steph   You and Nick, dear.

Lee   What about me and Nick?

Steph   I really thought you were my friend.

Lee   Yer are. What about me and Nick?

Steph   Oh, how much more bullshit have we got to take? Your secret's out, m'darling. Roy saw Tania and Wendy snogging, okay?

Lee   What?

Steph   I suppose Mike did have AIDS after all, but you had to hoodwink us into believing it was something else, just because you and your twisted little mind can't own up to being just a little bit human. I know you laugh at me behind my back but at least I'm honest about what I do. At least I can sleep at night.

Lee *punches* **Steph** *in the face, knocking him onto the couch.*

Roy   Ah, don't hit him.

Lee (*to* **Roy**)   What d'you have to go and say a stupid thing like that for?

Roy   Stop shouting at me.

Lee   I'll shout at who I fucking well like, now why?

Roy   Eh?

Steph   My nose is bleeding.

Lee (*to* **Roy**)   Why?

Roy   I don't know what you're talking about.

Lee   You *have* got a drug problem.

Lee *pours himself a drink.*

Roy   I've put me foot in it again, haven't I?

Lee (*to* **Roy**)   Have you got a cigarette?

Roy   I don't know. Probably.

Lee   Then give me one.

Roy   You don't smoke.

Lee   Why, Roy?

Steph   Oh, Lee, stop it, you know why. Because it's true.

Lee (*lighting one of* **Roy**'s *cigarettes*)   When? When did you see them kissing?

Roy   I don't know. Oh, yes I do. Before. Before I set fire to the balcony. There's not much damage.

Lee (*to* **Steph**)   See? He's barmy.

Steph   You just can't bear the fact that you've been caught out.

Steph *exits to kitchen.*

Roy   I'm sorry, Lee.

Lee   Oh, you will be.

Roy   It's just that I saw them kissing and me fag dropped out me mouth and went in the petrol and . . . oh, I feel fab.

As **Roy** *goes into an ecstatic trance,* **Lee** *goes and opens the balcony door. He inspects the burnt damage.* **Steph** *returns, nursing his nose with a wet tea towel and sits on the sofa.*

Steph   We don't care, you know. We don't care that you're getting your end away with him. And as for Tania and Wendy, well, yes, it does turn my stomach, but you know, I'm broad-minded. And even if Michael did have AIDS, so what? It's nothing to be ashamed of you know. You wanna be like me, practise non-penetrative safe sex. Simple solution. Q.E.D.

Lee *goes and punches* **Steph** *again.*

Lee   Get Wendy down here now.

Steph   Why should I?!

Lee   Just get her down here.

Steph   No, I will . . .

Lee *goes to punch him again.* **Steph** *rolls out of his way.*

Steph   I'm going.

Steph *exits.*

Lee (*to* **Roy**)   You did, didn't you?

Roy   I know. Eh? What did you just say?

Lee   You saw them. Oh, Roy. Was all that stuff about the dog crap?

Roy   You don't see white dog crap any more, do you?

Lee *sits down.*

Roy   D'you feel fab?

Pause.

I feel great.

Lee   Look, Roy.

Roy   What?

Lee   Do one, will you.

Roy   What?

Lee (*shakes his head, confused*)   Do one.

Roy   Another one? I've only got the one left but I'm saving it for later.

Lee   Go upstairs or something. Please.

Roy   Oh. Oh, okay. Okay.

Wendy *has just entered.* **Roy** *passes her to exit.*

Wendy   Okay, Roy?

Roy   I feel great.

Roy *exits.* **Wendy** *sees that* **Lee** *is smoking.*

Wendy   Put that out.

Pause.

Come on. Four months is a record for you.

Pause.

Lee. You throw a party to watch your favourite programme and then you spend all your time down here smoking. I wanted to go to the pub earlier, but I'm quite getting into it now. Some of those songs are really crass. Love City Groove are in with a pretty big chance I woulda thought.

Lee   I couldn't give a shit about Love City Groove to be honest with you.

Wendy   Now, come on, you don't mean that.

Lee   I'm afraid, Wendy, that I do.

Wendy   There's no need to get like that about it. Okay, so it's not as catchy as the usual entries but I don't believe for one minute it's put you off the Eurovision.

Lee   Nothing's put me off the Eurovision. Why, Wendy? Why?

Wendy   Why what? Put that out. You spent a fortune on hypnosis.

Pause.

Lee   I mean, it's not like I don't know how it feels.

Wendy   What?

Pause.

Lee   Look. Nick's my best mate. I love that lad. He's been like a brother to me since . . . I know things are dodgy between him and Tania. But. Why get yourself involved? Just. Wendy.

Pause.

Wendy   He's a bastard to her.

Lee   Kill it. Right?

Wendy   You don't know half the things . . .

Lee   I said kill it!

Pause.

Wendy   And what did you say to me at the age of sixteen when I couldn't understand why there was a fella in your bed? Eh?

What did you say then? Come on, lad. You've said it often enough to me mum and dad. Say it. Go on. Remind me what you said then, I've forgotten.

Pause.

'You can't choose who you fall in love with. If we could, the world'd be an easier place.'

Lee   I can't believe it.

Wendy   She's leaving him, Lee.

Lee   Why didn't you tell me?

Wendy   I've handed my notice in and I've got a job with a temping agency in Crouch End. Begin first of the month. Anyway, now you know. She's everything to me.

Lee   If you throw another cliché at me I'm gonna be sick.

Wendy   I'll be taking possession of a flat in Crouch End at the end of the month. Tania will be joining me just as soon as she sells up. So. I'll be able to pop round to see you as often as I like.

Lee   I'd like you to go now, Wendy.

Wendy   You've pigeon-holed yourself you know. I'm glad I never. At least I can go through life not regretting anything. You wanna really look at yourself.

Lee   Just go.

Pause.

Wendy   You're homophobic.

Lee   Oh no I'm not. You can call me what you like but don't you ever call me that. You should've told me. If that lad's feelings are . . . I'll fucking . . .

Wendy   What? Hit me? He hits her, you know. Your whiter than white best friend hits my lover. You're all the same.

She gets up.

Lee   No wonder you were so keen to come tonight.

Wendy You didn't think I'd come to see you, did yeh? Oh, what for? To thank you for pushing me round in a wheelchair?

Lee He'll be better off without her.

Wendy I believe this is mine.

She starts folding away the clothes-horse hanging from the radiator. She is beginning to get a bit manic. **Nick** *enters.*

Nick Oright, Wend?

Wendy Where's Tania?

Nick Gone for a walk. Clear her head, usual story.

Wendy Split up, have you?

Nick What? (*Laughs.*) No. No. I salvaged it. Again. Christ knows how long for. Christ knows why. Routine, I guess. Can't help but love me, warts and all, silly moo.

Wendy Pretty big warts!

By now **Wendy** *is hysterical.*

Lee Wend.

Wendy Oh, I'm Wend now, am I? Five minutes ago I was Wendy, now I'm Wend. There's progress.

Nick What's up?

Wendy You hit her.

Nick What?

Wendy Oh, so you're gonna deny it then?

Nick (*laughs*) Where'd you get that idea from?

Wendy . From my girlfriend.

Pause.

Tania.

Nick (*laughs*) Am I the only person at this party who hasn't taken drugs?

Wendy (*to* **Lee**)   Denial. He's in denial. Look at him, he's got it written all over his abusive face.

Nick   Grow up, Wendy, a joke's a joke.

Wendy   Oh, you gonna hit me now, are yeh?

Nick   Lee?

Wendy   Fraid I might report you to the police? Like she did? (*To* **Lee**.) Bet you didn't know he had a record as long as his arm.

Nick   What the fuck are you on about woman?

Wendy   I'm a lesbian! All right?!

Pause. Then **Norman** *shouts through from the bedroom.*

Norman (*off*)   I told yer she was! Didn't I say?!

Wendy   Oh, now he can just shut up.

Wendy *exits towards the bedroom. A lot of slapping and moaning is heard off.*

Nick   What's going on mate?

Lee   Oh, Nick. Nick. Come here. (*Draws* **Nick** *to him and hugs him.*)

Nick   Steph's got a broken nose, Roy's off his box . . .

Wendy *re-enters.*

Lee   Wend, what were you . . .

Wendy   Oh, shut up, he enjoyed it! Hey, what does a lesbian take on her first date? The removal van. Well, it's no joke. Now you were under the impression Nick that Tania was visiting her mother in Islington, well she was, but what you and her mother don't happen to know is that actually . . . I'm sorry . . . (*Almost crying.*) it'll all be fine and . . . just . . . just . . .

Nick *looks to* **Lee**, **Lee** *shrugs.* **Wendy** *bursts out crying.*

Lee   Oh, bloody hell, my heart's going. Feel that.

Nick   What? (*Feels* **Lee**'s *heart.*) Shit. Breathe. Breaths, big breaths.

Wendy (*to* **Nick**)   React! You bastard!

Lee   I had a line of coke from Roy and . . .

Nick   Come on, mate, just . . . breathe . . .

Just then **Tania** *enters carrying a tower of pizza boxes.*

Tania   I couldn't get out the bloody door. Which soft git ordered twenty quattro formaggio pizzas? Coz there's a geezer on the doorstep waiting to be paid.

Pause. **Tania** *puts the boxes down. She realises* **Lee** *is having some sort of anxiety attack and that* **Wendy** *is distraught.*

Nick? Did he order twenty pizzas from Pepino's Pizzas? That man's doing his nut.

Nick   I don't know.

Tania   Oh, for fuck's sake. (*Puts pizzas down.*)

The phone rings. **Nick** *picks it up.*

Nick   Hello? No, he's er . . . he's busy at the moment. What? Billy?

He puts the phone down.

Billy.

Tania   Well, what did he want?

Nick   He just said . . . 'Enjoy your meal.'

Lee   Tell the pizza man there's been a mistake go on.

Nick   Right.

Lee   Hurry.

Nick *exits.*

Tania   Wend?

Wendy   Crouch End.

Tania   Shut your big fat mouth, will ya?

Lee   I need a glass of water, Tania.

Tania (*pouring one*)   You've gone and blabbed. You stupid cow.

Lee   Steph told me.

Wendy   Steph?

Lee   Roy told Steph.

Wendy   Roy?

Lee   He saw the two of you kissing or something.

Wendy   Us two?

Tania   Keep going, Wend, you're working your way through every git at this party. You've only got Nick and Lee to go.

Lee   Steph of course, surprise surprise, assumed me and Nick were having a bit of a thing as well.

Tania   Yeah, well, Steph's the biggest arsehole going.

Lee   Not from where I'm sitting he isn't.

Tania (*to* **Wendy**)   You stupid cow.

Wendy   You've got to ring your mother.

Tania   Shut up.

Wendy   You told me to remind you.

Pause.

Tania   Cheers, Wend. Appreciate it.

Wendy   Crouch End. The swinging bed.

Lee   It's not her fault. She'da been quite content to keep it under wraps if you hadn't been seen.

Tania   Look, I haven't agreed to marry the bastard or nothing.

Wendy   He knows. I told him. Me and you.

Tania   Probably turned him on.

Wendy   He won't want you now.

Lee   I think I'm going to be sick.

Lee *runs off to the kitchen.* **Wendy** *tries to hug* **Tania**. **Tania** *shrugs her off.*

Wendy   You're a man. You do the sort of things men do. Fuck women up.

Enter **Nick**.

Nick   He's a pretty big guy. Pretty insistent. He's got a baseball bat down there. Wants a hundred and twenty quid.

Pause.

What should I do?

Pause.

Nick   Right, well, you can go and deal with him. (**Tania** *makes no attempt to move.*) Where's Lee?

Tania   Puking in the kitchen.

Pause.

Nick   She wasn't joking was she? (*Pause.*) Roy. Roy tried to tell me.

Nick *starts to kick the settee.*

Tania   Oi, watch it! Nick! Nick! Don't be a prize cunt!

Wendy   Don't say that word, Tania. You know it goes right through me.

Nick *looks at them. He starts to retch. He runs off to the kitchen.*

Tania   Christ, I said I'd ring me mum.

A fight breaks out in the kitchen, off. **Tania** *goes on the phone and dials a number.*

Wendy   What would she say if she knew what we'd been up to in the spare bedroom while she lay poorly?

Tania   Probably have a heart attack and die.

Wendy   Is my face a mess?

Tania   Shocking.

Wendy   I'd never hit you.

Tania (*on phone*)   Hello? Hiya, Paul, what you doing there? No, I've been out all night. Lee's.

Lee *enters from the kitchen with sick down his front.* **Nick** *is behind him. They are holding onto each other in mid fight.* **Wendy** *tries to split them up.*

Wendy   What the fuck are you doing?

Lee   Tell him. Tell him I never knew.

Nick   Tania.

Wendy   He was in the dark, Nick, I swear.

Nick   I want to hear it from her.

Wendy   Get off him, you battering bastard.

Tania (*on phone*)   Okay. I'll be over as soon as I can. (*Puts the phone down.*)

Lee   Me face, don't mark me face!

Wendy   Nick! Jesus! Me knee! (*Falling.*)

Nick   Tell him. And her. I never hit you.

Tania   Never.

Wendy   But the bruises!

Tania   I'm a psychiatric nurse for fuck's sake. I get manhandled!

Nick   She says you told her.

Tania   Well, that's bollocks then, isn't it!

Pause. **Lee** *lets go of* **Nick**.

Nick   Tell me. Tell me he didn't know.

Tania   Course he didn't. D'you think he'da kept silent with you?

Nick *lets go of* **Lee**.

Lee (*to* **Wendy**)   Nick wouldn't hurt a fly.

Wendy   I just saw the bruising and . . . Tania? What's the matter with your mum?

Tania   Oh, something and nothing. Had heart attack and died. Actually I better be going. Nick, you better run me to the hospital.

Wendy   I've got my car.

Lee   You've been drinking . . .

Tania   I don't care who takes me just hurry up. (*Getting stuff together*.)

Nick   No. I'll . . .

Wendy   I can . . .

Lee   Nick?

Wendy   I've only had a glass of Bucks Fizz. Which hospital is it?

Tania   They've taken her to the Royal Free.

Nick   I'm covered in sick.

Tania   Oh, come on, Wend, look sharpish.

Tania *and* **Wendy** *exit.* **Nick** *and* **Lee** *sit down side by side on the sofa.*

Nick   I'm sorry, Lee. Are you all right?

Lee   Yeah, I'm fine.

Nick   No, come here. (*Looks at* **Lee**'s *face.*) Let's have a . . .

Lee (*shaking him off*)   I'm fine.

Pause.

You moving in then?

Nick   I don't want to put you out.

Lee   If you were putting me out I wouldn't have offered!

Nick   Sorry. Yeah, why not.

Lee   Oh, Nick, I . . . I'm so sorry.

Nick   Bet I can say sorry more times than you.

Lee   Christ, Nick, don't you feel like hitting someone?

The ridiculousness of this strikes them both at the same time. They start giggling. The doorbell rings, three times.

Nick   Pizzas.

Lee   I'll talk to him. If words fail I'll call the police.

Nick   I can always do that. I've done four episodes of *The Bill*.

Lee *exits.* **Nick** *takes his shirt off. He rolls it into a ball and sticks it on the sofa beside him.* **Steph** *enters.*

Steph   They've been on.

Nick   Who?

Steph   Love City Groove. *Royaume Uni.*

Nick   Any good?

Steph   What do you really care?

Nick   Fuck all, I guess.

Steph   I don't like you.

Nick   It's no big deal. I'm used to rejection.

Steph   I don't like what you've done to our friendship. I don't like any of you any more. And if anyone's taking minutes let it just be said that I don't wholeheartedly approve. Anyway, Roy's just necked his second E and we are leaving. There's a bar in King's Cross which is showing the contest on a wide screen. Roy can dance his little tits off, I can watch the scoring. Leave you two to it. (**Nick** *raises a thumbs up and smiles.*) You probably think I'm stupid. Well, let's get one thing clear. I knew all along. You see, I can sniff trade at twenty paces. Just one thing, Nick. D'you feel guilty?

Pause.

Does he make you feel guilty?

He chucks **Nick** *the photo of Michael.* **Nick** *looks at it.*

Nick   He puts a smile on my face. Happy memories.

Steph   You can tell that boyfriend of yours I never wanna clap eyes on him again till the day I die.

Nick   I'm sure he'll crack open the Dom Perignon.

Roy *enters.*

Roy   Oh, here you all are!

Steph   Get your slacks on, we're going.

Roy (*to the topless* **Nick**)   Ah, haven't you got nice tits?

Steph   Hypocritical tits, that's what he's got.

Roy   Can I feel your chest?

Nick   For you, dear boy, anything.

Roy *sits next to* **Nick** *and runs his hands over his chest.*

Roy   Ooh, it feels lovely. You're dead straight-looking.

Steph   If you chopped him in half he'd have QUEEN written through him like rock.

Roy   Ah, you're lovely, you.

Nick   Well, I think you're lovely too.

Roy   D'you wanna come out and play?

Nick   No.

Roy   Ah. (*To* **Steph**.) Int he lovely?

Steph   How can a slut be lovely?

Roy (*to* **Nick**)   I love you.

Steph   No you don't. (*To* **Nick**.) He's on drugs, ignore him. (*To* **Roy**.) I'm getting your slacks.

Steph *exits to kitchen.*

Roy   I think he's jealous. He doesn't really mean it. I think he wishes he were you.

Enter **Lee**.

Lee   I think we better call the police.

Nick   Okey-dokey.

Roy   We've got to go. Steph said. Sorry.

Nick *removes* **Roy***'s hands and finds the phone.*

Roy (*to* **Lee**)   I always fancy your fellas.

Lee   Roy, I'll speak to you about this tomorrow. When you're a bit more *compos mentis.*

Roy   Fab.

Steph *enters with* **Roy***'s jeans. He throws them at him.*

Steph   Get them slacks on I want out.

Lee   Actually I don't think it's a very good idea to go down there just yet.

Steph   Hurry up, Roy. (**Roy** *puts the jeans on.*)

Lee   There's a brick shithouse of a queer-basher on the doorstep wanting the money for twenty pizzas.

Steph   You'll try every trick in the book to get me to stay, won't you. Well tough, we're going and that's that. Roy?

Roy   I've got both legs in t'same hole.

Steph   No, dear, they're in different holes.

Roy   Are they? They feel dead close.

Steph (*to* **Lee**)   I blame you for this boy's dependence on drugs. Roy!!

Lee   Roy, don't go down there.

Nick (*on phone*)   Police please.

Steph (*to* **Nick**)   Where d'you think you are? Sun Hill?

Steph *exits.* **Lee** *grabs hold of* **Roy**.

Lee   Roy. You don't wanna get hurt, do you?

Roy   No.

Lee   No. Well just stay here a second.

Roy   Why?

Lee   Just sit down.

Roy   I wanna dance.

Lee   Well . . . dance then.

Roy   Tar.

Nick (*on phone*)   Yes, we're having a spot of bother with a pizza delivery man.

Roy *starts to dance.* **Lee** *looks to* **Nick**. *Suddenly a scream of agony from* **Steph** *downstairs.*

Blackout.

Act Three

Steph is nursing a black eye on the couch with a bag of frozen peas. Roy sits nodding his head. Nick and Lee are drinking. Nick has put a top on from the clothes-horse.

Steph Not a big fan of the police. Borderline brusque if you ask me. If you ever do *The Bill* again, Nick, tell 'em it aint true to life.

Roy You oright, Nick?

Nick Yeah.

Roy Great.

The doorbell goes. Lee gets it. He hears who it is on the entryphone then presses the buzzer. Soon Wendy enters, out of breath.

Nick How is she?

Wendy Remarkably composed. She's in the car. Actually, she's asking for you. Wants both of us to go back with her.

Nick Where?

Wendy Your place.

Nick Both of us?

Wendy She knows it's cheeky but. You'd be on the couch.

Nick Where would you be?

Wendy Not sure yet.

Nick If you were in bed with her . . .

Wendy Aha?

Nick Could I watch? (*Pause, then tuts to* **Lee**.) Tell her I don't mean that.

Lee He didn't mean that.

Wendy I could kill a drink.

Lee You're driving.

Wendy   I'll stop off at an off-licence. (*To* **Nick**.) Coming?

Nick (*to* **Lee**)   I will go.

A derisory grunt from **Steph**.

Wendy   Me and Tania . . . well, you know that much. But these two aren't. (**Nick** *and* **Lee**.) Okay?

Steph   Losing you as a friend's no sad loss.

Wendy   Well, let's face it, Steph, there was never anything to lose.

Roy   Can you give us a lift to King's Cross?

Wendy   Sure.

Lee   Steph?

Steph *shakes his head*.

Wendy   Bye then.

Lee   Take a bottle of wine.

Wendy   Right. Can I take two?

Lee   Take the lot if you want.

Roy   What's meat got? It's got the lot!

Wendy *goes to kitchen*.

Lee (*to* **Nick**)   You gonna be all right?

Nick   I'll bring a car-load of stuff over tomorrow.

Lee   Phone me if you need to talk.

Nick   I'll hang onto this feeling. I might get to play a jilted lover one day. Hey, it's research.

Wendy *returns with two bottles of wine*.

Wendy   Roy?

Roy   Yeah.

Wendy   Nick?

Nick   Down in a sec.

Wendy (*to* **Lee**)   Bye.

Lee   Let me know the details of the funeral.

Wendy   Will do. Farewell, Steph.

Steph   I hope you crash and the pins in your knee get smashed.

Wendy *goes.* **Roy** *goes to follow.*

Roy   See you.

Lee   Ring you tomorrow, yeah?

Roy *goes.* **Nick** *goes over to* **Lee** *and hugs him. He starts to cry.*

Lee   Hey. Hey. Be strong.

Nick   I don't want to go. Make me stay.

Lee   Come on.

Nick   I'll see you tomorrow then, yeah?

Lee   Yeah, darling.

Nick *nods. He takes a deep breath then goes.* **Steph** *is left alone with* **Lee**. **Lee** *pours two brandies.*

Steph   Well, let's hope Billy gets his comeuppance. I should sue that pizza pillock.

Lee   Cheers. (*Hands him a brandy.*)

They clink glasses. **Lee** *puts his Eurovision medley tape back on. It takes a while for the next tune to start.*

Steph   Think I'll stop in and watch it on me own next year.

Lee   Yeah.

The song comes on. It's 'Love Enough for Two' by Prima Donna.

Steph   1980?

Lee   Yeah.

Steph   Sally Ann Triplett went on to be a member of Bardo in eighty-two. Still didn't win. You've got to admit. It has gone off. There's no novelty value any more. No dance routines. No skirt-ripping. Dunno when I last heard a boom bang-a-bang or ding

ding-a-dong. It's asking for trouble taking Euro into the twenty-first century. I want it to be like it used to be.

Lee I used to wonder if being gay was genetical. Something I'd got from my real parents. Or was it the way you were brought up, something I'd got from my adoptive parents. I finally decided it was just something I got from myself. It was just me. Something special. (*Beat.*) It still hasn't sunk in.

Steph Norman's still through there with Radio Two on. Fabulous bedstead incidentally. Very handy for the old handcuffs. Did you see that policeman's handcuffs? A marvellous feat of metalwork.

Lee Why don't you go in and finish Norman off?

Steph How can a master be bruised?

Pause.

Steph Where's the best place to get a cab round here?

Lee Kentish Town Road.

Steph Right.

He looks in the mirror. He inspects his eye.

If this comes up I'm not gonna get trade for months, am I?

Lee About time you had a rest.

Steph I hate Billy.

Lee I'll see him in court.

Steph Oh, before I go. Meant to show you this earlier. (*Gets photo out of his bumbag.*) Recognise her?

Lee (*studying photo*) She was in the New Seekers. Who's the little boy? It's not you!

Steph Bumped into her in a hotel in Scotland. Holiday. Eve Graham. She was ever so nice. Little poodle. I said, 'Shame you didn't win.' I must have been all of about eight. She said, 'It was rigged.' 'Beg, Steal or Borrow'. 1972.

Lee She's beautiful looking.

Steph   She had it all, didn't she? It's all ballads and techno now.

Steph *puts the photo away.*

Lee   See you then.

Steph (*knocks back his drink*)   Verged a tad on the prattish side, haven't I, m'darling?

Lee   What's new?

Steph   So long then.

Lee   Bye, Steph.

Steph   Billy'd be sick if he knew you'd seen that. (*Taps bumbag.*)

Steph *goes.* **Lee** *starts tidying up the debris. He switches the tape off and rewinds it. Suddenly* **Norman** *shouts through from the bedroom.*

Norman (*off*)   Norway! Norway have won! The bastards! I don't fucking believe it!

The tape comes on. It is 'Ding-A-Dong' by Teach-In.

Some soft get on a violona! There's no words! It's not even a song it's just a tune! (*Beat.*) My wrists are killing!

Lee *goes to his chest of drawers. He gets a huge whip out. He runs his hands over it.*

Norman (*off*)   Norway! Norway have won! It's not even a fucking song!!

Lee (*to himself, extremely angry*)   Oh, have they now?!

He brandishes the whip then whips the back of the settee. He looks to the hall door that leads to the bedroom. He looks at the whip. He heads off for the bedroom and shuts the door behind him. The lights fade and the music gets louder.